THE EARTHSPINNER

THE EARTHSPINNER

A Novel

ANURADHA ROY

HarperVia

An Imprint of HarperCollinsPublishers

THE EARTHSPINNER. Copyright © 2022 by Anuradha Roy. All rights reserved. Printed in the United States of America. No part of this book may be used or reproduced in any manner whatsoever without written permission except in the case of brief quotations embodied in critical articles and reviews. For information, address HarperCollins Publishers, 195 Broadway, New York, NY 10007.

HarperCollins books may be purchased for educational, business, or sales promotional use. For information, please email the Special Markets Department at SPsales@harpercollins.com.

Originally published by Mountain Leopard Press in 2021.

FIRST HARPERVIA EDITION PUBLISHED IN 2022

Designed by Terry McGrath

Library of Congress Cataloging-in-Publication Data has been applied for.

ISBN 978-0-06-322068-3

22 23 24 25 26 LSC 10 9 8 7 6 5 4 3 2 1

For Myriam

I'm bowl
And I'm platter
I'm man
And I'm woman

I'm grapefruit
And I'm sweet lime
I'm Hindu
And I'm Muslim

I'm fish
And I'm net
I'm fisherman
And I'm time

I'm nothing
Says Kabir
I'm not among the living
Or the dead

Kabir, sometime in the fifteenth century
Translated from the Hindi by
Arvind Krishna Mehrotra

ONE

Thursday, October 11

It is autumn and I am at university in England. I've never known autumn. Where I grew up, the monsoon cooled into a mild winter that the trees did not think it worth changing color for and in a matter of days it went straight to the infernos of summer. Here, the light is green and gold, and in the rectangle of trees framed by my window, russet and burgundy leaves drift from the sky, alive in the moving air. It's quiet enough for me to hear their soft rustle as they touch the ground and the nib of my pen scratching on blue aerogram paper. *I am fine, everything was okay on the plane. All the houses looked the same from the air, like toys. The grass is a different shade of green.*

"You always manage to get away, you always have it easy," my sister's voice keeps saying in my head. Those had been her parting words at the airport though she did not utter them out loud.

Tia has three years of school to finish, is defeated every day in her tussles with books. She can't get beyond 50 percent in any exam and cries, "What's the point of *reading* about gauchos and flamenco? I want to *be* in Argentina!" She has other plans for herself, ever changing save for one constant: they involve glass, not paper. Mirrors, camera lenses, dancing on glass, pouring cocktails into a glass. She has a low, rich voice, she has only to start her lazy humming of "Tall and thin and young and lovely" and people stop to listen. Her long, slender feet show that she has many more inches to grow. She wants to leapfrog over her school years and find youth, acting, filmmaking without the slog of a college degree.

"What do you mean, what's the news? Is there ever any news at this dump?" she wailed the other day on the phone when I called. "Now you've gone, I can never leave. I'll be stuck here, looking after Amma my whole bloody life."

"So much drama, Tia," I said. "Which book are you living in these days? Not *Little Women*, I'll bet. Where is Amma right now, anyway?"

"Still at work. And I'm busy too," she shouted, slamming down the phone. She'd be scowling and throwing punches at her reflection in the mirror next to the phone as if she were aiming her blows at me. Of this I was sure.

I spent the rest of the day sick with remorse about my sarcasm, picturing Tia in her room, music exploding through her locked doors while she skulked inside, hating me more with every angry yowl of electric guitar. Her door would stay shut till late at night and my mother would keep knocking louder and louder. "*Come out and eat, Tia . . . What's going on, Tia? . . . Tell me what's wrong.*" If I were home, I'd charge out for a run—needing to get away—whatever the time, however unbearable the heat.

I'm good at exams, but Tia is wrong, I didn't have it easy doing them and I don't have it easy now. I am broke here, on a scholarship that believes in enforcing virtue through austerity. The scholarship comes from the grandly named Farhana Abdulali Endowment for Girls' Education and is meant for Muslim girls. That didn't discourage Begum Tasneem Khan, who had her shrewd eyes trained on me through most of my final year at school though I did not know it. One afternoon I was summoned to the principal's office and I went in filled with dread but left clutching application forms.

"Why don't you apply," she had said. "No harm trying."

The people who run the scholarship are connected to her through a network of feudal relationships and I suppose her billowing magnificence ensured that they did not dare bring up the matter of my religion. Or they thought that my years in a Muslim school had made me a bit of this and a bit of that.

One of the interviews involved a dinner with the grandees of the city, watching like prospective in-laws, my mother said, to see if I knew a fork from a knife and could make vivacious small talk and laugh, but not too loudly. She advised me to stick to food minus wings and legs, so it wouldn't fly off my plate. When the day arrived, I could see Begum Tasneem on the other side of the dining table in the banquet hall, across a white battlefield glittering with silver and crystal. She was among many solemn people. She didn't look in my direction as the kind old butler whispered in my ear that I would be served each time from my left side, never the right. On his next foray he murmured, "Sit straight, child, take a napkin." I realized that the stiffly folded flowers standing at attention in silver holders were meant for use. I stole glimpses at the others and tried to be ladylike, delicately dabbing my lips every now and then, and restrained myself from diving under the table in panic when the napkin slid from my knees to the floor. Once the blur of chandeliers, silks, and silver had resolved themselves into particulars, I noticed a girl further down the table at the same instant that she puffed her cheeks, squinted her eyes, grinned at me, then put on her formal face again. We didn't exchange a word, but after that the evening became easier.

Weeks later, Begum Tasneem summoned me to her many-windowed office. I remember the blue glazed vase of spider lilies on her side table, the rows of group photographs on the wall, my hard-beating heart. The morning light, filtered by gauzy curtains, was behind her, giving her an otherworldly glow, and the air was perfumed by the lilies. The day had arrived. It felt as if I had been transported to one of those folktales where a god tells a bewildered human being: "Speak, what does your heart desire? It shall be yours."

Begum Tasneem's voice seemed to come from somewhere near the lilies and was scented by them. I had been given a scholarship to a grand university in England, I would have to go at the end of September, and they would take care of the flight too. The curtains stopped swaying and the light shimmered for a few seconds. Almost in the same breath, with an ironic smile, she said, "They won't let the scholarship go to your head, the endowment. They've measured out the money to make sure you come back educated—but also frugal, virtuous, grateful. A good girl."

Then she dismissed me with a wearily elegant motion which was both a wave and a gesture toward the door. "If I know you, Sarayu," she said, "you won't let a little bit of poverty get in the way of a lot of enjoyment." Her green-blue eyes, usually watchful and impersonal, seemed amused, and maybe she was even smiling a little as she returned her gaze to the open file in front of her.

Every part of the Farhana Abdulali Endowment is parceled out: the fees go straight to the university; dormitory bills are paid to the college; the rest must suffice for food and books and the occasional movie and is remitted monthly by an aged Abdulali who lives by the sea near Brighton. I have not met him, nor know how to reach him. Each time I cycle past the Japanese lanterns outside an enchanting restaurant on my route to lectures, or examine a noticeboard crowded with advertisements for concerts and plays, I want to tell him an extra hundred pounds would make not the tiniest difference to his life but would transform mine.

Abdulali austerity means there are times I don't have enough in the bank for a three-minute international call, and so I slip a fifty-pence coin into the phone box and wait for my mother to pick up the receiver and say hello. I know the call will disconnect immediately. She will know it was me, and I know too the place by the door, next to the long mirror, where she had to be standing as she answered the phone only to find the call cutting off. For the time it takes to breathe one breath, we are together, at two ends of a fine string across continents and oceans.

At the end of each day, if I can't make myself go back to my empty room, I go to the library, and if not the library I use a key I have been given to the basement of a church down the hill from my college. The basement contains a pottery studio, free for students to use if they have signed up for the ceramics society. I feel as if I've dropped into a secret cave through a rabbit hole—where the lights stay on, the kilns, tools, and wheels are tended by elves who do their work unseen, where stocks of material are magically replenished, and you can come in at any time of day or night. I've never known anything so luxurious.

For the hours I am at the wheel I don't have to deal with new people. I don't have to tell them what I am studying or where I am from or smile with pleased astonishment when they say they've always wanted to go to India. Besides, there is warmth, there is a kettle and tea bags, there is a tin always filled with fat, chewy ginger biscuits. The wheel turns, I place a ball of clay on it, I cover the clay with both my hands, and if I close my eyes I have the planet spinning in my palms to the hum of a motor. I don't want to leave the studio, I want to bring in a camp bed and books and be a hermit.

Tuesday, October 16

My solitude did not last. This evening, after only about a week in my cave, I could tell there was someone else there when I unlocked the door. I sensed a presence before I saw anyone, felt outraged, trespassed upon. Instead of damp earth, I smelled aftershave. I could hear the radio warbling, water gushing from a tap.

The atoms around me rearranged themselves into an unfamiliar pattern. I turned to leave. But the sound of water stopped and a voice asked if there was someone out there.

At first sight I was startled by the person who came away from the sink. I could see she was a girl, tall and slender, but her rolled-up sleeves revealed the shoulders and biceps of a young man. Her legs were planted onto the ground as if they had grown out of it, long and muscular. In the low-ceilinged basement where I've already got used to being alone, she filled the entire space. Then she smiled at me and I felt myself uncoiling.

She offered that smile but did not follow it up with words. She went back to work as self-assured as one who had been making pots forever. She took out three or four large slugs of clay from the store and kneaded them into one big lump, putting all her power into it, then cut it into slices with her wire tool. She went to the scales on the right-hand worktable and divided the clay into several six-hundred-gram chunks. All of this she did with a focus that blocked out her surroundings.

Once she had an orderly line of identical balls by her wheel, she climbed onto the seat and took a black-and-white scarf from a jeans pocket. I was trying to keep making whatever I'd begun, but it became more and more difficult to keep my eyes off her. She made a triangle out of her scarf and put it over her eyes, then tied a knot tightly behind her head so that she was blindfolded. After this she groped around for one of her balls of clay and started to center it, switching her wheel to a fast spin. In a few moments there was an improbably perfect shape rising in height between her seeing, feeling fingers.

The basement had begun to feel like a safe haven to me. With this tall, muscular, blindfolded stranger, it throbbed with an unfamiliar and menacing energy. The radio she had turned on played a song that urged everyone to always take the weather with them, but I can't see how that is possible if a single alien presence can alter a place this way.

Monday, October 22
Her name is Karin Wang. A different Chinese first name had been given to her at birth in Malaysian Borneo, but she hadn't cared for the sound of it and had shrugged it off. I carry my

old life around in an ever-present backpack that makes me ache from its weight while Karin appears to have sprung from the earth, unencumbered by parents, siblings, family, past. She's jettisoned all of that. "I am Malaysia's Olympic hope, that's what they call me," she said when we were next muddying our hands on neighboring wheels. This time she was working without her blindfold and had replaced her earlier silence with nonstop chatter. "They had a picture of me in the paper every time I won something. Golden girl, that's me."

Her father kept the cuttings in a scrapbook she never looked at. Her own scrapbook had pictures of airplanes, and she traced their shapes with her fingers, knowing that one day she would fly a long distance from the father who woke her up at dawn even on school holidays and took her to the beach where she had to run barefoot on the sand, as fast and as far as she could. He rigged up steel rings and bars for her to exercise on. Every morning she had to have two boiled eggs and salted fish while her brother tried not to look up from his small bowl of rice. Her father watched as she swallowed her vitamins, weighed her, and marked her height off on the wall.

"I'm something between my dad's guinea pig and a pig he's fattening, kind of, for the kill," she said. "I badly want to lose, but I'm too fucking scared of the bastard to do anything but win."

The way she spoke of him startled me. I tried to recall if I had ever been scared of my father. I could almost see him next to Karin, as if he really were sitting there and listening to her, his forehead furrowed with concern at her bad language. The same look he had with me and Tia through the last year or two when he was certain he did not have long to live and wondered if he could somehow make us grow up double quick.

Karin doesn't want to run or compete, she wants to study aeronautical engineering and fly planes. But her ticket to escape comes at a price: she is on a sports scholarship. She was offered a place, money, mentorship, coaching, even food allowances—as long as she keeps training for athletics medals and wins a few for the university.

"The further I run away from running, the more they make me run. If I don't run, I don't get to study," she said with something between a grimace and a grin. She dialed up the speed of her wheel so it flew into a blur and the wide-mouthed bowl she had between her hands spun crazily out of shape. She stopped the wheel and slammed her fist into the collapsing clay.

She is an unlikely presence in the studio. On the rare occasions that other students are down there too, they try not to stare when she strides in, muscles taut under neon tights which she wears with calf-length boots. Halfway through the door she starts shrugging off her dark green velvet coat, bought second-hand from Oxfam as I have discovered. Her hair is cut close to her skull apart from a fringe that falls down one side of her small, square face. Her nails have purple polish on them one week, navy blue the next, and before each session she goes through a ritual of removing rings from every finger, peering at her hands, and then biting the edges off her nails so they won't cut into the clay. I gave her nail clippers sometime after I met her, but I never saw her use them.

It turns out we are from the same college and if we cycle into town together, we go wildly fast downslope, drunk on the danger of it, hands off handlebars. Airborne. I never had the nerve to do that when I was on my own. One evening at rush hour, the bicycle pump strapped to my carrier fell off. I had shot forward by then and was too far ahead to know what had happened, but Karin stopped her bike in the middle of the busy road and held a hand up at the traffic. All the cars came to a screeching halt, she ran across to my pump, picked it up, waved a thank-you to the waiting cars, rode down toward me.

"If you pull this stunt where I come from," I told her, "I'll be scraping your remains off the road with a teaspoon."

Sunday, October 28
Where I come from. I thought I knew where I come from, what constitutes home. Home was my father asking us to be quiet because he wanted to listen to the cricket scores. It was the usual Sunday sounds of the newsreader's posh voice, the dissonant trumpets of a wedding band, my mother at her typewriter in her bedroom, the clacking of it a shower of pebbles, her fingers moved so fast. A time when Tia and I were still close, when any place was home if the two of us were together with the reassuring voices of our parents who quarreled out of old love.

Sitting here across the oceans, at this table where I can't see into the darkness beyond the disk of light from my lamp, I see a face reflected back at me in the window glass, and it is as if I am in the room but my face is outside, asking to be let in. I don't know this face. I need to work out how to reassemble myself.

It is fourteen months and eighteen days since my father's cremation. Afterwards, we found ourselves by the sea at the Gateway, and I say found because I can't remember how we got there or why we went, only that it was late in the evening, and there were many murky corners, and an elderly relative lecturing us about the need to be alert, to look out for pickpockets. It was windy. High waves crashed onto the walls and lovers leaned into each other when the spray from a big one burst upon them like a rain cloud. Men thrust screws of peanuts at us, junkies glowed briefly from flames lit under bubbling foil, then returned to darkness. Due east across the black water was Elephanta, to which my father had said we would take the ferry once his heart surgery was done—when he was out of the hospital, ready for a cricket match, as his surgeons had predicted. My father had three passions: geology, cricket, and ancient history. He had long ago stopped playing cricket, but he listened to the high-pitched frenzy of commentaries on the radio right till the day before his surgery. At the top of his list for after the operation was a cricket match at the Wankhede and a visit to Elephanta, because he could not tell which was more beautiful, a square drive by Gavaskar or sixth-century Hindu temples hewn out of basalt. His heart was a union of the two worlds and if he had made it to those caves, I was sure he would have pointed out stone gods positioned at slip and mid off.

I caught sight of my face a few hours after he died. It was in a hospital washbasin's scarred mirror and some of its scabs had become a part of my reflection, but otherwise I didn't look changed. I touched my cheeks to check if that unchanged face really did belong to me—because if body, heart, and mind had been one, my head would have been the crater of a volcano, boiling blood would have been spewing from it. I would not have had eyes to see my reflection.

As we stood contemplating the shadowy hillock on the dark sea, newly shaped by subtraction, my sister took my hand in hers. A whisper of a touch and it was gone, immediately doubtful. Our closeness had dissolved long ago and each day was a quiet war over trivialities. Her hand in mine that evening and my failure to hold it tight told me what nothing else could have.

Tuesday, October 30

My pigeonhole was spewing blue aerograms today—three came all at once, including a momentous one from Fauzia, telling me she's seen her first naked man. "Did it have to be a corpse on a dissecting table? A fat and hairy one at that, turning blackish-green I won't say where. This is what studying medicine gets you," she writes. "You're clever to have stuck to poetry and stuff. You get paid for having fun. Me? I've started smoking because I can't stand the stink."

Two of the letters are from my mother. That is unusual—Amma is not good at letters. I picture her promising herself she will write to me *that very day*, then remembering last thing at night when her eyes are too tired to stay open. I think of her writing to me early in the morning, resolute, scruffy-haired, reclining against the headboard, forgetting to drink her cup of thick black coffee in her search for words. "Now you're in England, studying English literature, I have to think through every sentence!" she writes. Then the scrabbling around for glue to stick the three flaps, putting the precious letter into her bag to post from work. Discovering in her bag the one from last week that she forgot to post. Unlike the glossy, sturdy aerograms you get here, the ones from home look worn and damp by the time they arrive and I have to be careful not to tear away her words as I slit them open.

Amma's letters tell me Tia has started staying back at school for guitar lessons, the chikoo tree from which our childhood rope-swing hung had to be cut down because of a fungus. Shirin Khambatta next door had terrible stomach pains and is in the hospital. "Who knows what's wrong with her," Amma says, "and the place feels even emptier without her across the garden."

From the five of us in the house it is down to three: Amma, Tia, the dog. I wonder how Dog is making sense of it—abandoned over and over again. I picture my mother armoring her heart against absences. She tries to write me amusing letters with gossipy snippets about the people she has met while gathering news, but her attempts at lightness don't always succeed. In her last letter she said she hadn't realized she was making up more and more questions and answers about absence, death, illness for the newspaper's weekend agony aunt column, managing which is one of her duties. Her editor had called her in. "Romance works better," she reported the editor as saying. "Love means hope and fun. Death is boring. It comes to everyone, love to a lucky few. No? Twelve inches less for heart attacks, twelve inches more for heartaches, and twelve months later we review circulation." My mother went back to her desk and asked her younger colleagues to lend her their love stories, supply marital problems to mull over. She was studying the intricacies of Mills & Boon novels as closely as I was reading Milton for my college tutorials.

When she went back to work after my father's death, I was still at home. It had been only three weeks. A colleague taking the bus with her, mistaking her stoicism for calm, said, "It was a shock, but you must be getting better now, aren't you?"

How to define getting better when you have lost someone you loved from the age of ten, whom you went to school with and college with, whom you married and made a life with? Getting better meant forgetting, and forgetting meant losing him every day afresh, and this brought about a complicated, exhausting battle inside her between the need to remember and the need to forget. She had tried explaining this to me but stopped short after a few minutes, when our eyes met. She returned swiftly to her typewriter.

These days, when letters come from home with news that no longer includes me, I feel as if I'm on a moving train and they are on another one traveling alongside, so that I catch a glimpse of Tia and Amma and for a moment, despite the noise, nothing moves, we look at each other from our separate windows. And then the storm passes and I am alone again, going further and further away from them.

There is nobody I can talk to about any of this at the university, not even my new friend Karin. Where would I begin? I am a sea creature transplanted onto land. I would have to start with explaining what water is. My tutor invited me home last weekend for grilled salmon and salad and I played with her infant children and their cats and when she asked, I said I was very well, thank you. If I said more, it would be as futile as telling the story of a dream.

Sunday, November 4
My days have begun to follow a rhythm independent of term time, tutorials, and friends, it's the calendar of the clay that determines mine. I think of shapes and colors waking and asleep, and instead of the books for my courses I keep reading about materials for making glazes and clay for pots. I've come across

names that ring small chiming bells inside me. Quartz, feldspar, limestone, dolomite. Cobalt, chromium, titanium, petalite.

I've heard some of these names before. They are like notes that linger from a happier time. I know about the Dolomite range and owe a visit to a companion of my childhood, *Piccole Dolomiti*—Little Dolomites—somewhere between Trentino and Verona, that my father told us about, wanting to share with us his fascination with the universe. Some evenings he went on reading aloud from books on geology, oblivious of the fact that Tia and I had tuned out in the first five minutes. But his voice seeped into us, and his oddly soothing discourses on plate tectonics, much of which we did not understand, collected in me and Tia and shaped us in the way limestone forms unnoticed in warm and calm seawater from sediments of shells and algae that remain in it as fossils. We would fall asleep to the sound of plates diverging, converging, sliding past each other, in the process causing new mountains to rise, oceans to churn, and continents to form or rupture. My father lived to only fifty-seven, but the time frames in his mind were made up of billions of years. In his personal atlas, Pangaea, Gondwana, and Laurentia were continents as real as Asia and Africa, and a fossilized ammonite, its spirals unspooling for millions of years, was not very old. One Himalayan fossil he found was shaped like a shell with waves of water on its convex side; in another you could make out a sea creature of some sort. He was fascinated by the idea that the Himalaya had been under water, peopled by marine creatures, only about sixty million years ago. By his side it was easy to visualize the collision of African and European plates in slow motion to the crashing sound of titanic waves, when mountains rose up bearing gasping fish and octopuses that would slowly petrify.

If sea creatures lived on dry land as fossils, I think now, my father too has merely gone into another element, somewhere I will find him again in another form. From warm living flesh he was turned to ash that we tipped into a river—and I thought that was the most final erasure of every trace of his physical self that it was possible to think up. But now that I am learning about glazes, I wonder whether he would have found it amusing or appalling if I told him I wished every now and then that I could turn his ashes into a glaze. Had he known that his rocks and fossils, even his own bones, could be used to color clay? If only I could reach into whichever element he inhabits now, to give him tea in my just-made cobalt-glazed mug. In the solitude of the studio, I find myself in conversations with him, asking him questions about my materials, seeking advice on melting points and fluxes. There are no answers. There is no one else in the basement, the other wheels are switched off. All I can hear are muffled footsteps in the church above and the staccato chatter of an electric kiln's thermostat.

Tuesday, November 6

Today I was alone in the studio. Weekdays, especially Mondays and Tuesdays, hardly anyone makes it here. I come in though, even if briefly, for the touch and scent of damp, pliable earth, which I need as other people need food and water. The feel of clay is the same everywhere, and this cave with tools and kilns is a piece of my childhood transported to a faraway place.

I haven't seen many other studios. All I know of pottery is Elango's shed by his moringa tree and his wooden wheel. In my new, cold country, the scent of clay is a way of traveling through improbable stretches of time and space to his low, turquoise-blue house set back in a beaten-earth courtyard and the auto-rickshaw rides to school during which he made up long and fantastical stories about the buildings, rocks, and river we passed.

He had been coming to our house for as long as I can remember, and his auto-rickshaw was a school bus for six of us in the neighborhood. One of the stories he liked telling the others was about the day he decided to teach me to make pots, when he came upon me in the quadrangle outside my house fashioning a duck from flower-bed mud. He would say with a flourish how he knew at that *very* moment he had to take charge of me or I'd lose the gift and turn into just another book learner. He would grin into the rearview mirror and say to Fauzia, "Book learning is for girls like you! Me, I never want to see a book again. You think I can't read? Let me tell you, I went to college and school. I know Humayun came after Babur and after him came Akbar. I can recite English poems. 'Twinkle twinkle little star, doesn't matter what you are.' Tables also. Five nines—ah what? Do you know? Let me see, is it sixty-three?"

Our chorus would follow: "Forty-five, 'Lango-anna, you don't know anything! You have the wrong answer again!"

The auto-rickshaw had a line of bells strung across the wind-shield that tinkled when we were moving, and when we gave the right answer, Elango ran his fingers through the bells to make them ring louder. He would groan theatrically at his ignorance, slap his forehead in comic gloom, go on to another topic in which he'd come out looking like a fool to make us wild with happiness. The gateman called ours the noisiest auto-rickshaw among all those that brought in brats to the school.

My father had seen Elango around when he was a boy helping his grandfather, who sold pots door to door. He came from a line of potters, earth-caked, sweat-stained, until his father forsook the unforgiving family trade for education and a clerical job and in due course introduced his sons to table fans, electric lights, books. There were days when my father watched Elango putter away in his auto-rickshaw after dropping us home, and shook his head in disbelief.

"That boy . . . he went to school, he even went to college. But he knew all his life he wanted to be a potter like his grandfather."

"Just like I know I want to be a singer, Appa," Tia would pipe up immediately. "School's a waste of time for people like him and me."

Elango had been to other parts of India to display the enormous terracotta urns he was known for, and even done a workshop or two for students at the local art college. A Korean potter he had met at a Delhi exhibition sent him a postcard every year, and—once—a beautifully packed set of tools and brushes. Elango sent him a fat, many-stamped envelope in return, whose contents he refused to disclose. His ties to the world outside his slummy neighborhood gave him the aura of a film star, but instead of capitalizing on his popularity he stubbornly carried on working alone, however little money that meant. He gave up neither his auto-rickshaw nor his street market stall, and he still loved nothing more than rooting around in a pond for clay, knee-deep in sludge.

"He's a crazy genius," my father said.

"So am I. You'll see!" Tia wasn't short of self-confidence even when pint-sized.

In the early days of my being taken in hand, Elango brought small balls of clay and showed me how to make things in a corner of the back veranda where he set up a wooden board with a basin of water. My father loved to watch him teach me. With the two of them staring at me and correcting me constantly I am not sure I ever made anything worthwhile, but when I was older, I started going to Elango's house to learn. He showed me how to prepare the clay before making anything out of it, how to wedge—to knead patiently until every bit of air had been pressed out from it. He showed me how his wheel worked. It lay at floor level and was made with wood and clay that was fashioned into a heavy disk balanced upon a grooved stone. He would turn the disk very fast with a stick and once it began spinning it was like a top: it straightened and kept spinning, I could not tell how. I would sit on my haunches and try to make small things on that big wheel. In the time I took to make one wobbly bowl, Elango would have a line of large pots beside him.

When I look around this basement studio, I want him to see it. It would satisfy his infuriating obsession with method, order, and cleanliness in the work space that made him wash or settle again each tool I used and put away. In this studio everything has its slot, hook, or shelf. Anything you might need is here. There are smooth and efficient wooden and metal tools. Electric wheels that hum softly, power that never breaks down. A big gas kiln that sits in the outer room like a shrine we are forbidden to approach. Buckets of glaze, and minerals and oxides we can help ourselves to if we want to make our own glazes. This is the West, it is a studio at an opulent university in the West, everything is for free, or almost, everything laid out for you. Yesterday a policeman smiled at me and said, "Lovely morning, isn't it?" He did not look as if he wanted to bash my head with a baton to pass the time. I was still wary. Like Elango I cannot let my guard down. Where I come from we have always known that ordinary days can explode without warning, leaving us broken, collecting the scattered pieces of our lives, no clear idea how to start again.

I have a diary of sorts from childhood because my mother scratched notches on the wall of our back veranda every birthday to measure our heights, Tia's and mine, and this wall was our demarcated scribbling zone, where we were allowed to draw pictures, dab paint. This wall was never repainted when the rest of the house was done, and against the notch for my tenth birthday is a penciled scribble in my mother's handwriting: "S—started with E," and against my twelfth: "S—potter's wheel." She must have known that year would always stand out for me. It was a significant one for Karin too, it turned out. Two planes crashed in Malaysia that year, she told me, and her best friend was in one of them. It haunted her, the thought of her friend's body falling from the sky into the sea. It was around then that she developed a fear of heights and an irresistible attraction to them, thrilling in the queasy feeling she experienced walking on the edge of sheer rock faces that fell to the sea far below, fighting back and simultaneously rejoicing in the thought that she could step off into oblivion. She wasted many hours by the ocean near her house the year of those crashes, peering into tide pools, thinking she might find floating parts of broken planes.

That was the year my parents bought our first gramophone with stereo speakers and a set of LPs, which turned Tia into a would-be rock star overnight. She knew immediately how to play air guitar and sing into handheld microphones conjured out of old tin funnels. She mourned for days when soon after—as if events are connected—Elvis Presley was found blue, cold, stiff, facedown in front of his toilet. Fifty thousand people died in a cyclone not far from us that year, and those who lived said they had seen flames on the ocean's waves. Snow fell in tropical Miami for the only time ever, and a Tunisian immigrant was guillotined in France for murdering his girlfriend. In the way chickens keep walking headless after they are slaughtered, the dead Tunisian's eyes looked around at the assembled observers for a long half minute and slowly blinked, well after his head had been separated from his body. Nobody was guillotined after this in France and the executioner's son, who had hoped to follow his father's profession, had to find other work, just as calligraphers and lamplighters have done.

It was 1977. There was jubilation in our country that year, which I was too young to understand, at Indira Gandhi's downfall. While our parents talked about an end to the brutalities of the Emergency, what interested me and my sister was Mrs. G.'s successor, a humorless old man who drank his own urine as a tonic. Tia and I sang a rhyme about the successor that went:

Dear Mr. Desai, would you like some tea?
Oh no, little girls, I'd love a glass of pee.

But more than my first pot, or anything else that took place in the world, what changed the configuration of earth-sun-sky in that year of unimaginable wonders and bloodcurdling horrors was the young dog that Elango found in a forest. The dog was black and brown, his ears were still deciding whether to flop or stand up, and he had a tail as curly as a comma.

TWO

I

Dawn. The windows are down and a dog hangs half out of a car, ears in flight, nose high in the air, gobbling the world with each breath. The woman has her eyes on the road, hands on the wheel. The man looks over his shoulder murmuring words that make the dog so frantic with love that he musters all the strength in his body to clamber over to the front seat. He sits on the man's lap, fixing his solemn gaze on the road. His coat is black and brown, his eyebrows chestnut.

Space expands. The horizon recedes. In the slow blooming light, adventurers in trucks, jeeps, cars have given the city the slip. Gray-blue sky, diesel air, pylons topless in mist. Bands of laboring cyclists they leave behind, men squatting behind bushes, ragged purple morning glory, far-eyed cows lost in thought. The woman presses down on the accelerator, thrusting all of that into the past. They talk, at times their hands reach out for each other across the seat, and after a while, soothed by the rhythm of the drive and their voices, the dog retreats again to the back.

Giant boulders stranded in fields. Huts you cannot tell apart from the mud. Circles of sky trapped in puddles, trees, trees,

trees. Bullock carts laden with coconuts, blue-and-white school-girls in pigtails. The sun stares into the car without blinking. Light-blinded, they drive through the day, crossing rivers strad-dled by crumbling bridges, towns that offer no temptation. The numbers on the odometer go into double figures, then triple. At dusk, they are still on the road.

The man is driving now and the dog begins to paw him and whine. Overhead is a green cathedral roof, and whatever light remains is sieved by the leaves. Though the city they are speed-ing toward is not far now, it does not feel that way on this road winding through stands of charred gum trees. Their trunks are black with soot, upper halves pale, jade leaves glowing. The dog paws the man again, more urgently. The man pulls over, throws back his head, closes for a moment his eyes that are bloodshot with staring into the sun. The woman springs out of the car with the dog on a lead. "Don't go far," the man says. He can see dim lights from a hamlet in the distance. His eyes follow the woman, who is urging the dog to hurry, but the dog, now in search of a scent, tugs at his lead and goes further into the woods. The woman's voice fades and birdcalls fill the emptied space.

Half-light fills the place with shadows as the woman turns back toward the road, but through gaps in the trees she makes out two men leaning in through the driver's window of their car. It must be that they are asking for directions, yet her heart turns into an iron ball slamming against her ribs. She sees the door open on the passenger side. In her nightmares she has been here often. She starts to run without movement, getting no closer to the car. She shouts, but her throat produces no sound. The car's door bangs shut.

The dog pulls the woman the other way, she tugs harder,

then drops the leash and runs toward the car uncaring. By the time she reaches the car, two men are dragging her husband out of it. He is limp. There is blood—the woman cannot tell from where—she hears herself scream, feels a rough palm flatten her mouth, is picked up, shoved into the car. She tries to open the door, but it is locked. The car lurches forward. She bangs the windows, claws at the face of the man next to her, who slaps her hard a few times and tells the bitch to shut her damn mouth or else. How to get out, how to get out? The thin man who has slapped her says with yearning that he hasn't fucked a woman for days, maybe weeks, he is ready to stick it into any roadside bitch or goat it's that bad. On and on he whines with the persistence of a mosquito. One of his hands pulls the woman's hair, the other gropes between her legs. A railway crossing comes into view and the man driving speeds up to race through before the barrier is lowered for a train.

The road is a set of craters held together with broken ribbons of tar, making the car jolt till her stomach churns, she thinks her bones might splinter. The woman can see the barrier is starting its descent, she can see a tractor and a van some distance ahead, slowing down. If the car stops at the crossing, she will cry out for help, she will escape. The thin man is saying he watched a rape scene just the other day. A gang rape, five men and the girl, and by God she could not stand on her feet by the end of it, they took turns, one from the back, one in the mouth and—all at once, the driver slams the brakes, leaps out, strides round to the back, grabs the woman and flings her to the edge of the road. She falls awkwardly. Her head hits something hard. A door bangs shut and the car vanishes into the gathering darkness toward the railway crossing.

What of the dog? Ran off toward the village? Or shrank into a bush, waited till all was clear, came back to paw the man and nudge him with his damp nose. Maybe. He licked clean the man's face and hands and the blood-smeared watch that lay by the man, returned to the split forehead, the pulpy eyes. When the man did not respond to any of his efforts to wake him, maybe the dog settled into the crook of his knee, as he was used to doing every night in bed. Scratched behind his ears, nibbled at a flea in the base of his tail. All that done, he tucked his nose into his paws and sighed with contentment at the closeness of the man. The chestnut dabs on his forehead patterned themselves into two alert faux eyes which said he never slept.

Things of this kind happen all over the world, every hour, perhaps every minute, more in some places than in others. The variations are infinite, and the particulars matter only to the people whose lives they touch.

2

I was just a girl then. I knew very little about the incident on the highway. I had only the bare bones from a newspaper report which ended in tiny italics with the name Devika Nanaiya. To other people she was a journalist; to me and my sister she was our mother, whose name in the paper was an occurrence so routine we often didn't bother to read her articles. Crime was part of her beat, and morgues, hospitals, and police stations were routine for her. She wrote of rapes, suicides, stabbings, and burglaries in a calmly factual style, laying out what was known, shorn of hypotheses. Tia and I preferred mysteries in books to those in her reports. But this one was different. There was a dog in the story.

The woman was not badly hurt, my mother's report said, though the doctors were not sure they could save the man. The criminals had not been caught and probably never would be; the stolen car most likely had fake license plates and a different color by now. My mother laid out statistics about violent crime, mentioned the missing dog, quoted parts of the commissioner's statement in which he had repeated the truisms the police kept handy for such occasions. A brief editorial agonized that the police were in the pockets of politicians and their mafias and predicted that such crimes would become so commonplace that nobody would bother to report them.

My father put down the paper with a shrug. "The village near the level crossing . . ." he said. "The place is a kindergarten of petty criminals. Den of vice. Good thing you mention that Narsimha was the kingpin. Guns, hooch, people—what didn't he trade in?"

Tia drew her idea of vice from a movie we had seen recently—*Sholay*—snappy lines and dancing barefoot on broken glass till you bled. "I want to be a kingpin too," she declared.

"You'll just be a queenpin," I said. "They'll paste you on a dartboard for practice."

I was only eleven but already a cynic about the things people let girls do. Besides, dens of vice didn't interest me. They were everywhere, you could hardly walk out of home without stepping into one. What I wanted to know was this: Where was the lost dog?

3

A horse was in flames. It roamed beneath the ocean breathing fire and when it shook its mane the flames colored the waves red and when it erupted from the water it was as tall as a tree and the fire made the crackling sound of paper. It towered above the low-roofed house Elango lived in. The flames were at the hooves, the long solid cannons, and as they reached the muzzle, he worried that the horse would burst from the heat. Had he remembered to leave an outlet? Anxiety forced its way through his troubled sleep and all at once his eyes were open.

He lay still, elbow propping his head, dazed by his dream, needing no clock to tell him it was just three in the morning— the hour of wakefulness for petty thieves and born worriers. He shut his eyes again to see better his burning horse and understand what it could mean. By dawn the hens would start their clucking and crowing and his brother's wife would resume her daylong monologues with them, cooing at them to come and get grain, coaxing them to lay more eggs. The time until then was short, it was his own, and he wanted to stay suspended in his dream, clinging to its fading threads.

He got down to work on the horse that very morning. In singlet and shorts he tramped through Kummarapet to the scrubland a short distance from their house, down to the pond from which he dredged clay for his pots and idols. When this wasteland too was given over to a landlord, his pond and its surrounding soil would be gone and with it his clay—he knew this was the future. His grandfather had worked with the earth from here and dimly in his memory his great-grandfather before that. His grandfather had told him when he was a child why the neighborhood was named Kummarapet: because of their ancestors, the potters—the *kummara*—whose village it used to be. If you cut me open you will see clay in my veins, his grandfather used to say. From earth to earth was for him an inheritance. But their thriving workshop was long gone and there was only Elango at the pond now, though most of the clay he needed had to come by truck from a supplier. It cost money, and he could not raid it to make his horse for fear of his older brother noticing.

Often Elango thought that if—as people liked to say—God was a potter, then He had spun him and his brother to life on different wheels, from different earth. "No problem, no problem" was Vasu's favorite expression. Not for nothing was he a tout at the magistrate's office forever devising ways for people to dodge property surveys, fudge application forms, forge documents and jump queues. If there was a rule, he knew how to find a way around it. His eyes would gleam, he would scratch his oiled scalp with his pen and say, "Just relax, sir. You have a problem, I have the solution."

Where Vasu was a walking calculating machine, Elango hardly bothered to add two with three, and the earthen lamps he made, the gods and goddesses, the humdrum things like water pitchers, curd pots, flowerpots, and tea glasses that he sold in stacks to wholesalers—these wouldn't have taken him very far. His main source of income was Sudhakar, an old college mate who now designed the interiors for a chain of hotels. He ordered terracotta urns from Elango for the gardens and lobbies of the hotels. It was he who had pulled off a place for him at the national exhibition in Delhi, and enthusiastically promoted Elango's pots at hotel exhibitions. When the two of them sat and smoked together over a rum and water, Sudhakar would say he wanted the world to know great artists here lived in poverty and yet made extraordinary things. "Somewhere in the muck there has to be a lotus growing," they would chorus. It was something one of their college teachers, Mr. Murthy, was given to repeating as he ran his eyes despairingly over the class full of boys he called loafers and rascals, and even as they grinned at their shared memories, Elango was sometimes surprised by his friend's spontaneous affection. His own quieter sense of Sudhakar being the brother Vasu never was made him feel a little guilty.

Elango's urns were monumental enough, and timeless, but the terracotta horse came from a past more ancient, a place deep inside him where memories and stories lay waiting like a rich seam of clay. In his dream the horse had risen on its own like an earthen fountain. It wore a necklace of beads and its ears were like two mango leaves on either side of its magnificent head. On its forehead there was a design that he couldn't yet clearly see. On its back was a tasseled saddle which led to a tail that flew like a flag. The mane swept down the neck in a wave, the eyes stared straight ahead, gazing at eternity. Elango knew his own horse would not satisfy him if it did not match this dream animal.

He hunched over the bed of the pond with his spade and crowbar and began to dig. The mud was green with slime in places. Closer to home was a smaller pond on which waste floated like a slow-moving patchwork sheet. But where he was digging now, like his forefathers, was the potters' pond, a store of earth from which gods had been made always, and superstition threw a wall around it that no bricks could. It was clean and drew birds and insects. When the sky above had a few clouds and a soft breeze bent the rushes on its banks, it was as if the pond had been there since the earth began and the same bone-white egrets had picked their way around it even then.

Today there was not a cloud in the flat blue sky. October, but you would think it summer. It was hard, hot work and his singlet was soaked with sweat, but he felt energy and hope coursing through him. His dream had meant something. The horse was both sign and envoy, telling him Zohra would be his, but he would have to work to make that happen.

4

For how long had he lived with Zohra in his head? He could not be sure anymore because it felt as if it had always been so. She and her grandfather had probably moved into the neighborhood at the end of the last winter, almost a year ago. Elango had not noticed her at first though he must have seen her around Moti Block, the scabby gray tenements above the shops where she and her grandfather lived. That whole year now felt like lost time: crazy not to have stored away those glimpses for sustenance.

Imprinted in his mind was the day the turmoil in him began. It was at the weekly street market when she stopped at his stall. Their hands had touched when reaching out for the same lamp.

"It's very pretty," she said.

"When you light it, it will cast the shadow of a flower," he said.

"Really? A rose or a hibiscus?" she asked him in an innocent voice. Even as he was wondering if she was making fun of him, she picked up another pot, removed its lid. She raised her eyes to him questioningly. Brown, he noted, their rims filled with kajal.

"It's for setting curd," he said. "The best curd—there will be no water swilling around."

"The best curd because it's the best pot with the best lid?" She looked up at him with a mischievous smile, and then quickly down again.

After that she had said something about the dolls too, he had no recollection what. The impish smile had been fatal. He knew he wanted to listen to that voice, see her smile for hours, days, years, his whole life.

The next week she had come back—why? What was he to her? She had come again not to buy a pitcher but because she had felt something stir inside her too—he wanted to believe this, and by degrees it grew into a certainty in his mind. He tried to make sense of the way everything shifted that day for Zohra, as if a stage had been swept clean, the curtain raised, for her to occupy the center.

She was in sunset yellow and a gauzy pink dupatta that trailed over her shoulders. There was a tiny blue pendant at her neck.

"The lamp which makes the shadow of a flower when . . ."

"Yes, yes, there it is," Elango said. He wanted to give it to her. He wanted to give her all he had on the table. She could have anything, she had only to ask.

She reached across the table for the lamp and her dupatta slipped down to the crook of her elbows. He caught a glimpse of deep shadows between curves in the moment it took for her to right her clothes, and this she did promptly, with a swift apologetic look at him. He noticed the patch of sweat that darkened the yellow fabric at her armpits, the narrow wrists, the cleft chin, the leathery mark on her right arm that must be from a burn. As she walked away, he saw her hips moved oddly because of a limp. Something about that limp undid him. He felt himself sucked dizzily into a spiral of longing and lust from which he knew he would not free himself.

One waiting customer, a woman with a gold nose stud poking into each nostril, said, "Is anyone going to tell me the price or do I need to be eighteen again?"

He hardly heard her although he answered her with practiced ease. "Four rupees, Amma, but for you, because it's the best evening of the year, it is two only."

There was nothing he could do that day other than steal glances at Zohra as she made her way among other stalls down the street lined on both sides with peddlers shouting themselves hoarse about the superior quality of their clothes, toys, kites, food. There were two others with clay goods and people were bargaining so hard he could not leave his stall for a moment to slide away after her. And if he did follow her would he ever return? He dragged himself back to the business of earning. But from the next evening he took to visiting the Moti Block shops for a smoke if he saw she was there buying rice, millets, sugar, oil. To stand next to her for a few minutes, pretending not to notice her, even as he directed every atom of mental energy inside him to make her stay where she was—a little longer, five minutes more. Three minutes. He could not gather the courage to nod at her, or find a word to say. When he chanced upon his reflection in shiny car windows he did not like the face that looked back at him. Why would she?

Zohra did not come back to him with a single gesture that would have given him hope. He began to think he had misread her. Or that, like him, she had lined up the facts of their lives, turned them over carefully, seen the intractable problems, then quelled her feelings for him. She had succeeded where he had not.

For months now, he had done little but dream of her and there was nothing else he could do, knowing it was hopeless. She was the granddaughter of a well-known calligrapher, he was a potter in a place that was no longer village nor fully town, just a place that had been left behind as the city grew around it. "I'm neither this nor that," he groaned to Sudhakar, the only friend in whom he confided. "Not a fancy artist who can buy up the world, nor an illiterate village potter who wouldn't dream of dumb impossible things."

"Just a pig-headed one," Sudhakar said. "You could be rich if you made what people wanted. Do some shiny novelty items. Tutti-frutti colors. Diversify."

Elango shook his head. "It's terracotta for me, you know that. It's honest."

"Yes, yes, yes, I've heard that old story before," Sudhakar said.

Elango was apt to be loquacious and plummet into sentimentality after a few drinks, but even sober he thought of this as a kind of truth that applied to pots as well as people. "I mean it," he said. "Break it whichever way you want, it's the same all through."

He didn't dare tell Sudhakar he also rejoiced that since terracotta was cheap, the poorest household could afford his pots and pitchers. But this meant his hands had often to be soiled not with clay but with grease: in his spare time he repaired pumps, sewing machines, stoves; he ferried people in his auto-rickshaw. His encounter in Delhi with the Korean potter who had invited him over was ancient history and the tools and bamboo brushes he had sent were memorials Elango did not use for fear of spoiling them. A faded stack of books was the only remnant of his education, while Zohra even now studied Arabic with her grandfather. The only reassurance was that she was almost as hard up as he—calligraphy was as outmoded as handmade earthen pots.

A morning came back to him when he had seen Zohra out on the narrow strip of a veranda that ran along the front of her tenements. He was waiting in his auto-rickshaw for a fare when she appeared just above him. Through the last few months of observing her at the grocery store he had seen that she regularly bought grain for birds and that morning she was reaching up for a pot suspended above her parapet and filling it with bajra. The mild sunlight of the early hour touched her from somewhere indefinable and lit up her hair. She closed her eyes and raised her face to the morning sky. Just then, out of nowhere, he felt a whirring gust on his face, a wingbeat on his shoulders, and from the corner of his eyes he saw an emerald shape flash past him. When it landed on her parapet he realized it was a brilliantly colored bird almost as big as a crow. It sat there for a moment and then it hopped onto her outstretched arm. She did not open her eyes or move a muscle and her palm cupped with grain remained motionless. He watched transfixed from below. The bird paused for a few seconds to eat, then was gone. Zohra opened her eyes and carried on filling the hanging pot with bajra as if nothing remarkable had happened.

But it had happened. And so swiftly that when he thought back he wondered if he had dreamed it. He never saw the bird again. He saw dun-colored sparrows, mynahs, crows, and bul-buls come to the balcony, but never again that bird, whose colors grew more dazzling in his mind's eye as the days passed. It had come from nowhere and touched him with its wings before landing on Zohra's arm. It had picked up dust from him and taken it to her. Over the next days, his glimpse of the mysterious bird came to feel like a sign in a language he could not understand.

He wanted this sign to bring him the only message he yearned for, one that would tell him the unbridgeable crevasse between him and Zohra would one day close, the earth would heal itself, and he would be able to walk across to the other side where she was waiting for him. What divided them made it unthinkable for him to tell anyone other than Sudhakar about her. At night he sometimes rehearsed the words to himself as if he were breaking the news to Vasu: "There is a girl I like—she is . . ." And then despair would eat up his words. He could not utter what she was, a Muslim. The space between the two was a charnel house of burnt and bloodied human flesh, a giant crack through the earth that was like an open mouth waiting to swallow him.

He could not imagine a life without Zohra. That was unbearable. But he dared not imagine a life with her. It was inconceivable. He told Sudhakar this.

"Give up the idea," Sudhakar said. "In this country it's just film stars and cricketers who get to marry whom they please."

"You bastard, I thought you were a friend . . ."

"I am. That's why I'm telling you, give it up."

"Wait . . . there was someone even in my locality . . . Aslam, my father's age. Remember, I told you he ran off with a Hindu girl from the next lane."

"Yes, and what happened after that?"

Elango said nothing. What had followed was a routine written in age-old stone: both Aslam's father and the girl's brothers had sworn they would kill the pair the moment they returned. Nobody had seen them again.

Even so, no harm dreaming. At night he lay awake, as he had done the night before and the one before that, listening to the rumble of his brother's snores, which were loud enough to roll out from inside the house to where Elango slept under the open sky in the courtyard. Some days he was daring enough to think he had Zohra sleeping next to him and it made him worry that he too might make these piglike sounds while she, slumbering, would be a serene goddess. Looking into the dim shadows, he felt her beside him, her head on his chest, breathing into his slow-beating heart. Gently, tenderly, his fingers went through her long hair, sending her into deeper sleep. When she woke up, she turned to him. And turned to him again.

5

He sat down at his wheel every day because there was work to be done, though his heart felt like a slug of clay, heavy and cold. When it didn't come alive, neither did his hand on the wheel. He felt distracted and debilitated. Stoically he bore his sister-in-law's tirades about sloth, or walked off mid-lecture for a glass of whatever it was they called rum down at the corner.

When thoughts of forbidden desires came close to tipping him over the edge he tried to think instead of the terracotta horse of his dream. He recalled from his first year at college wizened old Murthy Sir, in whom the diesel fumes of the present became the ancient air of myths and sagas with the scent of brine and wood and fresh-cut grass. Murthy, gnarled with the weight of learning, wagging a futile finger at the lust-filled boys in the class and telling them how Lord Shiva's passions had begun burning up the universe. To calm him and to save the earth, the gods placed his fires in a mare's mouth, then took the mare to the ocean. Under the water the mare burns quietly still, Murthy had said, it shifts and moves with the waves, it turns on its side and drifts toward the ice caps slowly consuming the ocean, waiting for doomsday, when it will be released during the final deluge.

The more Elango thought about his dream the more it unsettled him. Lust, doomsday, destruction, they had nothing to do with his love for Zohra. Old Murthy had told them about Achilles, Paris, Helen, Hector, a Trojan horse that had spewed soldiers in the dead of night. Perhaps that was a less fearsome myth about his own predicament. A potter trapped in an epic of his own, a woman at its center, two blighted lovers, their union thwarted by warring tribes. But who could he hide in his horse's hollow clay belly to go with him into the battle that was to come? He had no army. He had never felt so alone.

He had seen the ceremonial horses made by his grandfather long years ago, which were taken around the village in an annual procession. It struck him that he could make Zohra a horse like those, but also not like them. Not a cunning subterfuge nor a restless omen below water nor a sentinel. It would be their wedding horse, a steed for a man to seat his bride upon and sweep her away into a gold-and-red sunset. The horse grew grander with every imagining. The word would spread. People would come from other places to see the work of this brilliant potter whom nobody had thought to notice until now, and with them would come Zohra and her grandfather.

He was often wrapped up in his thoughts and he smiled, frowned, gesticulated, even muttered to himself. It took an explosion of curses from his brother to bring him back to the present.

6

Elango came back from the pond that afternoon and settled down to smoke and draw, leaning against the trunk of the moringa tree in the center of their courtyard. In some seasons, hundreds of caterpillars came and took up residence on the tree for weeks, invading their rooms, getting into their clothes, leaving fiery trails of itches in their wake. Eventually, caterpillars covered the entire moringa trunk so that the tree wore a live hairy carpet, and when they saw that, the two brothers started a fire below its trunk and watched the smoke and flames lick at the caterpillars until they peeled off the tree and fell into the fire in slow-writhing clumps. The air smelled of burning flesh. Caterpillars gone, the flowers turned into green sticklike fruit that was their food for many days. Some years there was so much they had to sell the surplus.

This annual ritual was one of the few things that brought Vasu and Elango together. The other was Vasu's unspoken, grudging admiration for his brother's work. Though Vasu pretended to scoff and was caustic about Elango's earnings, he did handle the sales, the middlemen, the clay supply. When Sudhakar showed Elango's work at a hotel exhibition, Vasu, dressed in his best, walked from one piece to the next, proclaiming their beauty as if he were a visitor who had just discovered a genius. "If only I had the money, I would buy this urn immediately," Vasu liked to sigh, peering like a connoisseur, clicking his tongue, shaking his head in theatrical sorrow, hoping his performance would encourage other people to reach for their wallets.

The memory of his brother at the exhibitions made Elango smile as he picked up a pencil. He sat cross-legged below the tree and with quick strokes sketched a horse, drawing it as a way of not forgetting. Before he started making it, he would sketch it many times more, and in sections, so that he had it clear in his head before his hands touched the clay. The eyes and ears were hardest to visualize, the jaw and the length of the nostrils were no easier. The tail came without too much thought. He made five diagrams, tearing out two pages in which his horse had turned into a creature somewhere between a dog and a pig.

Until Revathi came out and said, "Are you going to bring wood, or will you sit there all day?" His brother's wife liked ordering him around in her loud, grating voice, as if she were Vasu's deputy, and he took care never to obey right away. She stood in front of him with her hands on her hips, blocking the light.

"Forget wood, I have a better plan for today," he said with studied slowness. "Shall I tell you?"

She picked up a broom and began to sweep with violent energy, glowering and muttering as she directed dust clouds in his direction. Ignoring her, he drew his horses steadily for another five minutes and only then got to his feet. He picked up his axe from its corner, felt its familiar weight, and heard in his ears the *"hunh, hunh"* explosion of his own breath each time he lifted it to split a log. He thought how it might be to bring it down instead on a vicious woman's neck.

7

It was an hour to the wilderness that in his grandfather's time stretched from the border of Kummarapet. Over the years the woods had retreated, cut down for buildings and roads, and even after traveling so far, Elango had to dodge forest guards, coming back empty-handed some days.

The trees edged closer to each other as the light faded. The guttural chatter of monkeys died down as birdcalls filled the air. Crickets chorused for the time it took to breathe twelve breaths;

stopped as inexplicably as they had begun. Then there was silence but for the repetitive call of a solitary bird. Elango could not make sense of these things. For long minutes he forgot what he had come here for and stopped in his tracks, wondering why the chirping of crickets began, what made it end, why did the mournful bird call so mournfully—could it be for another bird?

Tying up his last bundle of wood, he heard a different kind of sound, something between a whimper and a cat's mewing, then saw movement near the bushes a few yards away. He froze.

Another of those sounds, closer now.

The guard on his rounds? A dacoit? A forest god disturbed at his wood being cut? The shadows of trees in the evening drove rational thought from his mind. He looked around, stepped backwards, then sideways, peering into the darkness. Seeing some movement, he gripped his axe tighter.

It was a dog.

A young dog and it had stopped in its tracks. When Elango took a step toward it, its curly tail wagged.

"You little runt," he whispered. He slapped his forehead more in relief than annoyance, laughed out loud.

The dog's paws were brown with mud and it was mud-spattered all the way to its elbows. Where it was not muddy it was black in color though it had chestnut patches above its button-round eyes, like eyebrows. It was not a wild dog. Elango could see a collar round its neck, a muddy leash trailing from it. Abandoned, very likely, by people from the city. Rich people very often left unwanted puppies in wooded places distant from their homes. The bewildered castaways scrounged at the shacks and stalls by the level crossing, sometimes thrown scraps but more often than not kicked around until they were run over by a train. This one was not a newborn pup, though it was not old either, maybe a few months.

He picked it up. Below the mud its paws and chest were the same chestnut as the eyebrows. He flipped it over, saw a pale mark on its chest that was shaped like lightning. Or like a Z. He looked between its hind legs. A male.

That made certain things a lot easier.

He contemplated leaving it in the forest. But now it was pawing him and licking him.

How can I leave it here? It'll be dead in a day.

So what? That's a dog's life.

This is not a dog, it's a puppy.

Are you going to keep it at home? A big sahib with a pet dog, is that what you are? Take it away from this forest and drop it near a rich house. It can live or die.

He scrabbled around for one of the burlap sacks he kept in the back of his auto-rickshaw and, after shaking out all the bits and pieces of twigs and dung from it, put the dog inside. As he struggled to fasten the squirming bundle to one of the auto-rickshaw's rods, the pup stuck its head out of the sack's opening and nipped him with its needle-sharp teeth.

"Watch it, you," Elango snarled. "Or I'll dump you right back in the forest."

The dog shrank and Elango felt himself forced into a gruff, conciliatory tone. "Don't do that again. Just sit in there, okay?" He tied the leash to the rod between the two seats.

Driving now, he glanced occasionally toward the dog at the back even as he looked for a suitable drop-off spot. The first stretch was too lonely, then came the railway crossing with the tea shop where he could see two big dogs . . . they'd tear this thing apart. He drove on, getting closer to the city. High-walled suburban bungalows, but he couldn't see a watchman to leave the puppy with. Could it be left outside a locked gate in the dark? It would wander off, get run over in no time. He needed to find a place quick if he wanted to get home at all, but the stretch where boulders were piled on boulders was next, possibly jackals lurking. Then came the bridge over the river, no good either, and so it went on until he found himself turning downslope toward Moti Block, and passing it, looked out as always for Zohra. Maybe that was her—waiting on the veranda that ran the length of her tenements. He saw a flash of blue and pink in the light of a bare bulb dangling on the veranda and stopped for a minute, pretending to check on the dog. Looked up again. And there she was, turning the other way, as if unconcerned. When she went in, he carried on, elated now.

"That's a lucky sign, I'm sure of it," he said to the dog in the sack. "First you, then her . . . you saw her too, didn't you?"

The puppy's head was like a pom-pom at the top of the sack, his tongue hung out from the side of his mouth, and his eyes were glazed with fear. Elango turned away from him. Signs were all very well, but what the fuck was he to do with this damned pup?

By the time he got home it was late and he was hot and annoyed with himself for having wasted the entire evening over a stray when there were a hundred things to do, a horse to be made. He tied the dog in a corner while he stacked the wood and finished his chores, washed in a hurry, and sat down to eat.

There was much that he disliked about his sister-in-law, but her food—unlike the woman—was irresistible. She had only to stir things around in a pan for them to turn into a delicacy, though his brother oozed bile where others salivated, always claiming to find too much salt or too little. That was just Vasu being Vasu. The slow drip of his bile soaked the courtyard by nightfall each day. After the customary complaints, he went around switching off the lights, muttering about wasted electricity. Elango switched a light back on to annoy him. He sauntered off and sat cross-legged on the veranda floor hunched over the newspaper his friend Giri brought back every day from his office. As casually as he could, he said, "Leave that dog there. I've got to keep it tonight."

Vasu peered at the tied-up pup and shrugged. "I have a full day's work tomorrow, unlike some. If there's a sound from it, it's finished, understand?"

The small whines from the dog were soon lost in the background noise of the neighborhood. The overture of Vasu's nightly snores. The radios, the clang of pots and pans from neighbors, the high-pitched sobs of the young widow next door who squabbled violently with her sister every night.

Elango gave up reading and lay on the veranda trying to block out the cries, fanning himself with the paper. Inside was a table fan, but inside were also his brother and his snores. Mosquitoes circled him but did not sting—he was one of the lucky few on earth whose blood mosquitoes found distasteful. Gradually the mosquitoes gave up, the heat ebbed a little, and the sounds died away though the sobs lingered for a while. He sighed and luxuriated in the nighttime quiet. It did not last.

The puppy started with soft whimpers, then whined louder and the cries rose till they seemed to pierce through everything. He mewled and squealed without pause until Vasu burst out through the door, yanked at the leash that tied him, picked him up, and flung him into a far corner of the courtyard. There was a soft thud, a yelp, then silence. Moments later the dog resumed his high-pitched cries, now more piteous.

Elango straightened his aching legs and got up to find him. He scooped up the cowering dog from near the moringa tree and tied him to one of the poles that held up the thatched roof of their veranda. He lay down beside him. Vasu would arrive any moment if this went on. Why didn't he just leave the blasted thing in the lane outside? It wasn't as if he usually even noticed animals. There was no shortage of dogs and puppies on the streets, and he hadn't bothered with any of them. What switch had this one turned on inside him? Was he going soft? A woman. A horse. Now this dog.

"Chinna, Chinna," he crooned to the dog, whose cries of sorrow became fainter and more forlorn as the night passed. He kept stroking its back and it moved something deep inside him that he did not know was there. He found himself murmuring half-asleep, "Chinna, this is your home now. I'll look after you." The dog whimpered and pushed his nose into Elango's hand.

What are you doing, you fool, how will you keep it with you?

But how can I push it out there now? It won't last ten minutes alone in the streets.

His hand went on stroking the dog even as the quarrels inside him continued, becoming more garbled with drowsiness. Despite the subdued whimpering, his exhaustion deadened his limbs, his hands paused on the puppy's back, and he fell into a bottomless, dreamless well of sleep.

He shot up in the middle of the night with the thought that he had given the dog neither food nor water. He slapped his forehead, scolded himself in a savage whisper. "What did you think, you dunce, is it a doll? Will it live on air?"

He crept into the kitchen. There was no milk, no dal, nothing that Elango could see in the half dark. All the food had been eaten but for a dried, charred roti nobody had wanted. They always ate rice, why had Revathi chosen this of all days to make rotis? He came back to the dog and lay down beside him. He tore a piece off the roti and held it toward the dog, who stretched an inquiring nose at it, took it into his mouth and gnawed, then spat it out between his paws, uneaten.

"It is too hard for you, you're still a baby, you should have milk with it, but I can't find any," Elango whispered. "Wait."

He put a piece of the roti into his mouth and, as the dog stared with anxious eyes, he chewed it to a mush, spat it into his palm, and held it out to him. The dog licked his palm with frantic attention. Elango chewed another mouthful and then another, feeding the dog until the roti was finished.

8

The name Chinna stuck. Elango didn't have to think about it, his tongue formed the word whenever he saw the thin, eager, bright-eyed dog and he called out to him with a tenderness he wasn't aware of possessing. When he took him anywhere away from their courtyard, he strung into the dog's collar a rope longer than its leash so that he could tie him securely. It was necessary. On his wood-collecting round a week after finding the dog, he had lost him for what felt like hours. One minute Chinna was next to him, the next he was gone. Elango had searched every part of the forest, wood and axe forgotten, calling his name even though the dog did not yet know it was his name. He found the dog sniffing a patch of ground right next to the highway, pawing it and whining as if to dig out a bone. Elango scolded him gently and picked him up.

"So close to the road. What if some car comes and runs you over? Was this where those bastards dumped you?"

On his knees he examined the hole Chinna had begun to dig. "What have you hidden here? A stash of gold bones . . . ?" he whispered, scanning the ground. His eyes caught a glint of something shiny, he picked it up and turned it over. A wristwatch. Someone had dropped it. The dog sniffed it, gave it a few licks.

"Who dropped this, Chinna? Someone you knew?"

Absently Elango patted the dog, rubbing the dirt away from the watch. He had never held anything so expensive before. It had a leather strap and in the dimness of dusk the numbers glowed green, pointed to six forty. His own cheap watch had died long ago and he had forgotten how it was to have one. Strange to be told the time in the middle of a forest—now that he thought about it, he had never needed to know it here. He relied on the sun and the crickets and birdcalls. Would he ever wear this shiny watch? Vasu would ask where he had got it. He would assume Elango was earning more than he let on, stashing away the money. He would take the watch away as if it were his by right.

He put it on. "Clever Chinna," he said, running his fingers over the dog's soft head, gazing admiringly at his wrist. "You've found a good luck charm. And you found me. And if you're driving me crazy, it's not your fault, is it, you little devil?"

The dog cocked his head at the man, bright-eyed. As Elango turned over the watch and examined it, the dog settled at his feet and busied himself gnawing at the edge of the man's trousers.

Elango saw that the watch had tiny English words engraved

in a circle on its back. He could make out the words, *JM to ZM, in love, May 1976.*

What were the chances of the initials on the back of the watch containing the letter Z? There could be no clearer sign that everything was working to bring Zohra to him, the sky was raining signs. He was troubled for a fleeting moment that someone who had been given the watch as a token of love had lost it—but he did not want to ask himself too many questions about whose it might be or how it had ended up there in the forest. It was waiting there, alongside Chinna the dog, and this was what people called destiny. Best to embrace it and be grateful. Mysterious things happen in this world, we cannot know it all. This was what his grandfather had believed and handed him as a natural inheritance. Look at you now, Elango said to Chinna, we can't explain what brought you to me, what kept you alive in that forest all alone until I found you. But here you are and if you leave again, I know I'll be done for. The wise knew better than to analyze every single thing, Elango told his dog. Nobody could explain how one year, when a solar eclipse darkened the afternoon, the mute daughter of the stonemason had spoken for the first time, asking why night had come early. At first the mason thought he was hearing things—then realized he was. She went on talking for a full five minutes after that, unaware she was a sudden sensation. Maybe in her head the guttural sounds she had made all her life had been words. The girl could not tell the difference and prattled on, oblivious of the miracle. After the eclipse, she banged the doors shut again and didn't say a word for another week—then, just as people were dismissing her brief spell of articulation as freakish, she had announced, "Look, that boy is going to be hit by the bus." And he was knocked down on the road the next day, as she had foreseen. Now there was no stopping her. She made so many alarming and often accurate predictions that the mason said in despair they had been better off when she was mute. Where was the explanation for any of this? Tearing open a marigold to find its secrets destroyed it altogether.

This was Elango's conclusion as he hid away the watch, and he repeated it to the dog off and on. Chinna had brought him good fortune. His life had changed. His heart felt bigger, more alive, as if a clear spring had exploded inside him and soaked a parched wasteland crying out for water. Flowers had bloomed, new blades of grass. The desert had blossomed into a garden.

9

Chinna sat on a square of hard earth close to Elango while he worked, staring at his surroundings, occasionally snapping at flies. The monotonous clacking of the potter's wooden wheel made the dog drowse off at times, but little movements or sounds only he could discern would make his head shoot up. His mismatched ears, one up and one floppy, would prick, his eyes would dart around while his nose tried to detect what was at hand.

It was in this way that he first noticed the hens that Vasu's wife kept. There were seven hens and three roosters. They crowed every morning in a cracked voice, setting one another off. In certain seasons the hens laid so many eggs that Revathi made enough money for her to fill three of Elango's earthen piggy banks which she hid in the kitchen. The chickens were let out from a ramshackle wire coop twice a day to scratch the ground, strut around, feed on scattered grain. Chinna was afraid of the rooster, because it was roughly the same height as he was, and it snapped at him with its sharp beak, but every day he sized up the red hen that looked slow and fat. He had chased it a few times and each time it had escaped his clumsy paws in a rush of wings.

Today he saw the red hen a few yards away, pecking and pocking and picking its way straight toward him. He scented success. Chinna lowered his tousled head, crouched on the ground, and waited as motionless as a mountain leopard for its prey. The hen tapped a leisurely way toward the dog, absorbed in its search for food, when there was a sudden flapping of wings, a wild squawking, and to his amazement Chinna had her between his paws. He looked around as if wondering if the bird of his dreams was truly his. It screeched for its life. Revathi shot out of the kitchen, saw the captive hen, picked a stick up from near the door, and lunged for Chinna, who caught the blow on his rump and yowled in pain. The dream was over.

Elango's wheel spun awry, the wet pot on it wobbled, then fell. He leaped to his feet, grabbed the stick from the woman's hand, raised it over her, his head on fire. He slammed the stick into the side of the wall. It splintered.

"Next time you touch that pup . . ." he growled. He said no more.

Revathi did not wince. She stood with her chest heaving, eyes popping with rage, nostrils flared. Her eyebrows drove a flat, angry line across her face. "Next time you threaten me," she said, "I'll break every bone in that cur's body." She held his gaze for a while, then turned around with deliberate slowness, leaving him holding his broken stick.

That evening, when Vasu came home from work, he went

into the kitchen for his glass of tea, came out shortly afterwards, and said, "I'm giving you a week. Either that dog lives here, or you do."

"It's my house too, you can't order me out of it," Elango said in an even voice. "I will live here, so will my dog, and if I have a woman someday, so will she."

Their voices rose. Old accusations were dredged up from the past and flung about. Over the low wall that separated their house from the one next door, they heard Akka scoffing. "Three dogs are bad enough and now there's a fourth. All barking, pissing, shitting . . . Look at the flies!"

Elango always turned a deaf ear to the voice over the wall, but at the mention of the dog he snapped. "Shut your mouth, you foul old witch. Go back to your spells and potions."

"If that dog steps anywhere this side of the wall there'll be a potion for it too. That potter who thinks he is so clever should know that," she screeched back. "I've dealt with more than a few curs in my life, I can tell you. They lift their legs against every wall . . . Fools. Let's see how long this one survives."

Akka, as she was known around the neighborhood, was thick with the priests at the temple nearby, she burned incense and rang her brass bell to God every evening without fail. She charged a small fortune to chase away spirits, foretell futures, cure herpes, or cause it. Her powers allowed her to adjudicate in neighborhood politics, forbid marriages or settle them, approve or kill deals in the making with a doom-laden prophecy or two. Conversation with this neighbor had ceased years ago but that did not stop her constant threats, observations, invective. The roots of the old estrangement were tangled, ever-growing, ever-evolving, and she flung accusations over the wall about stolen land or hinted at vendetta. She could make life difficult for those she disliked. The dog was a convenient pretext.

Elango thought it through while preparing his clay and decided the best way to protect the dog and his own sanity was to keep acrimony at bay. He shackled Chinna nearby when at work or if he had to leave the house briefly or when the hens were out of the coop feeding or when Revathi was in one of her moods. Much of the day the dog ended up being tied, fretting, whimpering, pawing the ground. Elango's heart contracted to see an animal bursting with innocent energy imprisoned all day. He knew it could not go on this way for long. Now that the school holidays were about to end he would be out all morning with his auto-rickshaw on the school rounds. The dog could not be left in the yard. A spell of time alone, a chunk of poisoned meat tossed over the wall . . .

This last thought came to him in the middle of the night, as always at three, and he went from asleep to awake in a second and groped for the dog. He was right there, whimpering in his sleep, and his vulnerability froze Elango with fear. Beyond the circle of his arms around the dog were Akka, Vasu, and Revathi, the rushing city, the forest with its jackals. At that moment he thought the dog, more than Zohra or the horse, had unlocked something in him that unnerved him with its power. There came times when his feelings caused him to ache in his chest, and then the fear of losing the foundling made him hold the dog closer, babble a silly patter to him, consulting him on questions to do with his pots and clay and the woman he was in love with. He had not known there were so many words inside him.

Chinna twitched in his sleep and his paws cycled in frantic, futile chase. Elango stroked him back to calm and buried his face in his soft, sweet-smelling fur. "Nothing bad will happen to you again. I'll keep you safe. I'll do whatever I have to."

The next morning, he revved his auto for the first day of the school term, lifted Chinna up onto his lap. It was early, just seven, the morning air still cool, birdcalls punctuated by bells from Akka's favorite temple. The three buffaloes from down the road were being let out of their dung-plastered pen. They made their way to the quadrangle Elango was heading for, ambling black mountains that blocked the width of the narrow lane. He swerved ahead, one hand holding Chinna tight against his stomach, and steered his way down the three lanes that separated down-at-heel Kummarapet from houses with gardens. Two of the girls he ferried to school lived there.

The father of the girls he had seen around for years, from the time he was a boy selling pots door to door. The mother was a short woman with cropped hair, looking in her usual brown pants and white shirts like a policewoman, but she was the caring sort, he knew from experience. Besides, for some years now, he had indulged the older daughter's passion for making things with clay. From crude ducks and rabbits, she had progressed to simple pots on his wheel. That made him her teacher. It was time, he thought, for this lot to be asked a favor, they owed him one.

IO

And this was how Elango's Chinna came to us from where he lived, a few lanes down from us.

Our house was one of eight grouped around a quadrangle which my father remembered as a big garden. The garden and the bungalow in its center had belonged to my grandfather. My father had memories of living in it until it was knocked down for new houses built by a landowner everyone called Taatha. In Telugu it is the word for "grandfather." He must have had a real name. I never knew it.

In our minds Taatha had always been old and always wily; he watched out for weaknesses, then swooped and made a kill. My father told us how his own father, never wise with his money, had become Taatha's kill before we were born. Taatha kept track of every financial crisis my grandfather found himself in and lent him funds against his land and the bungalow that stood on it. Neighborly loans, my grateful grandfather had assumed. Loans my grandfather could not pay back in the years left to him, Taatha knew.

Land grab in his bag, he knocked down the old house, promising my grandfather one of the new ones he would build there. He arranged them around a dusty yard, four houses staring down the other four. They were made to the same plan: double-storied, four or five rooms, and two deep verandas with flagstone floors. Shared wells in small, shared gardens. Ours was the only single-storied sand-colored house, fronted by a cool gray-stone veranda. Three stone steps led up to it, and then to our front door.

That October morning, when I answered the door ready for school in my green tunic, I found Elango holding a little black-and-brown dog. He put it down and immediately the dog began straining at his leash. The next moment he was in my arms. He licked me all over while his tail kept time like a metronome. His sharp teeth dug into my hand when I held him too tight. I must have shrieked—Tia and my mother rushed out to look.

"Amma," Elango said in a wheedling tone, "this is my Chinna. People treat him badly when I'm not there. My brother's wife can't bear the sight of him. Will you keep him while I am out of the house? Just a few hours."

"How can I have a dog here? I am at the office all day. Definitely not." Amma sounded severe, looked at her watch. I held my breath. I knew how dangerous it was to make her late, trap her in long-winded questions of dog-sitting when she had to get to work.

"He doesn't ask for anything," Elango said. "You can leave him in the courtyard. He will be safe here, that is all."

"Please, please, Lakshmi is here when you are not, please say yes," Tia begged. Amma frowned at her in the way that usually stopped us in our tracks, no matter what. "I need to think about it. We can't rush into this."

"What is there to think, Amma?" I cried. "It's for a few *hours*!"

I picked up the pup and even as he licked my face, Tia grabbed him from me. "It's my turn," she said, pirouetting with the puppy in her arms.

"Be careful, Tia," Elango said, picking up one of my clay creations that was drying in the sun on the veranda ledge. "Wasn't it two hours it took for Sara to learn how to shape this pot?"

My mother's assessing glance traveled from him to us, and the look that passed between them as he put my pot back on the ledge contained a map of our relationship marked with all its signposts: his visits to our house as a child, how much my father liked him, the hours he spent teaching me, the years of taking us to school.

Tia was now hopping on one leg, squealing, "Sara, it's not

fair! You've held him for twenty whole counts and I had him only for nine!"

"If I can't find a place for the dog, I will have to stop driving my auto-rickshaw till he grows a little . . . I cannot leave him alone at home when he is so small. Only a matter of a few months, Amma. Once he is older, he can look after himself."

We scented success. We knew the story of the camel and the tent and we knew our mother well. She was a chocolate truffle in human form, her crust hid a soft, melting center.

Tia kissed Chinna's head. "You will live here from today! You are mine!"

At this Elango said, "It is only for a few hours while I'm out with the auto-rickshaw, and if your mother allows. I know this is a lot to ask."

He took the dog back from Tia and set him down at my mother's feet, waiting. His gaze had an intensity that could make you think he was staring. But he wasn't—this was how he always looked at things which mattered, when every atom of his attention and intelligence was concentrated on something, pot or person. But the battle was already as good as won. The dog's small tail was going round in circles as he pushed his nose into the hem of Amma's trousers and she crumbled before the three pairs of eyes focused on her.

"Stop that," she said, in the direction of her feet, picking up the puppy. "It tickles." She was still at the door when we left, holding the dog with a look on her face that said she was happy but wasn't going to admit it.

Elango bundled us into the auto-rickshaw and turned the corner. He dropped off his cargo at two different schools. Fauzia, Tia, and I got off at Safar, perched on a rise just before the walled city. As soon as you crossed the river that cut the town in half, you saw the white domes of our school. We had about half an hour till we got there, and once the three of us hopped off, the other three went a little further to St. Teresa's. It was a long journey and because Fauzia and I were very little when Elango started taking us to school he had begun the practice of diving into an inexhaustible treasure chest of stories for us to while away the time. The chest had hardly been depleted over seven years of being raided.

Once long ago, his stories always began. Once long ago, a deaf, mute child started to speak during an eclipse. Once long ago, the fires of Shiva's rage had to be stored in a horse that still walks the ocean floor, breathing out flames. Ships sailed in this river we are crossing and they brought silken bears and tigers with eyes of opal. Geography and history were transformed daily during our journeys with Elango. He put lost lovers into buildings we passed, placed werewolves behind boulders. He filled the world with orphans who became film stars in Bombay and girls who shot off to the moon on rockets made in Sivakasi.

Today his story was going to be about a potter and a dog.

II

One of Elango's stories was about Laila and my grandmother.

Long ago, when he was a boy, his daily work was to wander the streets with an old man, selling pots from door to door. There was no auto-rickshaw, they had a donkey. The grizzled man who did the rounds with their donkey was perhaps a relative, but Elango was not sure who the man was, or where he eventually disappeared. He was one of four or five men at his grandfather's workshop in the old days. His shoulders had developed a hump with long years of work and his hands had twisted up with arthritis so he could no longer make pots. Instead he had been given the work of loading water pitchers and flowerpots onto the donkey and taking her around.

The donkey was small and pretty, and Elango called her Laila. She was fitted with ropes and a burlap carrier and stood still as the stack of heavy clay pots on her back grew until she was half-hidden under the load. Then they took her down streets deserted in the heat, slapping her forward. Elango's job was to call out to people to come and buy. He had a shrill singsong cry which he repeated as they walked. *"Kundalamma kundalu, naanyamaina kundalu, manchi neeti kundalu!"* Pots for sale, sturdy pots! Pots for sale, water pots!

One such day in summer when no one seemed to be interested and the donkey's load had not been lightened by a single pot, they were about to turn back when a woman in one of the bungalows opened her gate and called them in.

"This was your grandmother. It happened before your father was even married," Elango said to Tia and me.

"Are you thirsty? Is the donkey thirsty?" my grandmother asked Elango. "What have you eaten since morning?"

Elango stood mute, taken aback by her questions.

My grandmother repeated the words louder and slower, smiling encouragement at the speechless child looking up at her, mesmerized—though she had no way of knowing this—by the shadow of a mustache on her buttery face.

At that we fell against each other in the back seat of the auto, giggling. Elango grinned in reply in the mirror, and went on.

The hunchbacked man pushed the boy aside and stepped

in. "Amma, we have been out all day, from dawn, no rest." To emphasize his suffering, the man let out a soft groan as he slid to the floor of the veranda and sat on his haunches.

She told them to wait and had a servant lay banana leaves onto which he ladled steaming white rice, two kinds of vegetable, and sambar. Only once at a wedding feast, Elango said, had he eaten so much. After they had finished and were ready to leave, my grandmother pulled out a money bag and paid for each of their pots, double the price they had asked. As an afterthought she said, "Leave the donkey here, it's old and tired. It is time for all of us to beg its forgiveness." She fished out more money from her bottomless purse, waved a hand at her servant to deal with the donkey, and went back into the house.

Laila had been standing at the gate, head bowed. Flies buzzed around her shanks and she flicked her tail to drive them away, but that was her only movement. The servant who had brought them their food summoned a helper and the two of them pushed her toward the back garden, pitchers, pots, and all. My grandmother had not bothered to look at the pots.

Once it was in, they shut the gate. Elango said he was so confused by everything that had happened, he kept looking at the gate waiting for the donkey to return until the hunched man grabbed his arm, dragging him away, clutching his fistful of money. "I'm old and tired," he mumbled. "I wish she had bought me too and kept me in her garden! Never in my life have I so badly wanted to be a donkey." He kept chuckling and sucking on his teeth all the way home, squirreling away some of the money into a hidden pocket at his waist. Before they reached Kummarapet he threatened Elango with the Black Death if he ever spilled the beans on how much the woman had paid.

There was a picture of my grandmother at home and after hearing Elango's story Tia and I placed my father's magnifying glass over the smiling upper lip to find the mustache. There was no evidence of it in the old photograph, which had been touched up with pale spots of pink on the cheeks and blue and gold on the sari.

My father said he did recall coarse hair on his mother's face and he confirmed the presence of a donkey in their garden, remembering its fringed eyes and the quiet sounds with which it had munched the grass of their lawn, mowing it smooth for quite a few years. If not for my grandmother's flamboyant gestures of generosity and my grandfather's absentminded ways with money, my father added, we would probably have had our old, big bungalow still. His tone was factual rather than nostalgic, and he returned to his book without giving the matter further thought.

12

This dog they were saddled with now, Devika said to Raghav, could it be the one the couple in the forest had lost in the attack she had reported on a few weeks ago? Didn't he remember— when the car had been stolen, the man left for dead, the woman beaten up—there was a lost dog? The more she thought about it the more likely it seemed.

Her husband was half-asleep when she spoke into the darkness. He mumbled something about coincidences, turned over, and was gone, leaving her alone with her worries. Troubling ideas had a way of tormenting her on the brink of sleep. It was what came of working late at a newspaper office: the news turned into lice crawling nonstop through her scalp. She had gone with a photographer to look at the scene of the car hijack. A long drive in the trundling office Ambassador watching the road unspool as it left the city, when she tried not to be distracted by the rushing air, the unaccustomed loveliness of massed trees. She made notes. They stopped at the nearby tea shack to ask questions, spoke to the railway lineman on duty. She was told that the woman had found her husband more dead than alive on the side of the road. The two of them had stayed stranded until at dawn a half-empty bus to the city stopped for them. So much blood, the passengers in the bus had cried out in horror—and then the woman had broken down. The man had opened his eyes in the hospital after three days struggling for his life and the first thing he said was "Tashi," calling out to their dog.

An ordinary dog, the woman had said to every stranger in the next few days. Brown and black, with pale markings above its eyes. It had on a red collar with bells, and a leash. It was about six months old. Could it be a coincidence, thought Devika, that Elango had found a pup of about that age and that description around the time the woman had lost one? Could he have bought an identical collar for his dog? It had to be the same dog. It ought to be returned.

She lay staring at the ceiling fan, writing a letter to herself. She grappled with every kind of problem for her newspaper's weekly agony column, *Ask Mrs. Vanamala Reddy*. She offered resolutions to dilemmas in a tone that struck a delicate balance between unsentimentality, matronly solicitude, and humor. On weeks when incoming letters were too few, she devised both the questions and the answers. Except now she had no answers for her own questions. Her letter grew longer, and like a tangled ball of wool, the problem became knottier the more she tried to untangle it.

Sara and Tia were besotted with the dog. They came home from school and rushed to him. Chinna did a demented dance in return, rolling in the earth, digging holes, and rushing away to bring the red ball they had bought him with their pocket money. His coat was softer and shinier now, his body was filling out, you could no longer count his ribs with your fingertips. Elango would wait with a look of bemused adoration on his face to take him home.

This had become a daily ritual, Devika told the ceiling fan. It wasn't fair to an animal to toss him from one place to another. That couple would have to get another dog.

She fell into a troubled sleep halfway through the night and woke early, in a bad temper, the spokes of her hair a porcupine's quills. She felt like one too. She stood on the back veranda that abutted the kitchen, nursing a cup of coffee so thickly black she knew it would make her feel ill, but she went on sipping it.

From where she was, the house next door could be seen across a garden with a well at its center. They shared the garden with Mrs. Khambatta, a recent tenant who was still practically a stranger and Devika saw the woman sitting on a chair on her veranda, drinking from a mug. She had a newspaper open on her lap, a pen poised over it, probably for the crossword that Devika's tetchy colleague, the yellow-toothed Mr. Seshadri, concocted every week. "Hound—, Elvis Presley song (3)" he had set as one of the clues that week, since connecting the crossword with current events was what he considered his especial genius.

Mrs. Khambatta felt Devika's eyes upon her, put her pen down, and called out, "Early bird! Good morning! Come, have a coffee!" Devika gave her a quick smile, raised her cup to show she already had some, and ducked back into the kitchen. It was the end of her morning solitude.

The daily flurry of the girls being reunited with Chinna ensued and once Elango had driven off, Devika saw the dog sniffing near a clump of cannas in their backyard.

She called out in a furtive hiss: "Tashi, Tashi."

The dog raised his head and looked at Devika as if he had heard a word from a dream. His brown eyes shone, his tail started wagging, he flicked his ears forward and back. She swore at herself in a savage undertone, placed her coffee cup on the kitchen counter with a thump that should have broken it, turned on her heels, and shut the door.

Later that day at work, peeping over the shoulder of the paste-up artist in the design room, she grew queasy with worry. The man was sticking a photograph into one of the advertising boxes that appeared on the last page of the newspaper. He turned back to look as he sensed her behind him. "See this? First time I have put in an advertisement for a dog. Lost on the highway."

She stood at the bus stop later that day, too distracted to climb in when her bus came. She started walking, reached the bridge, paused to look down into the river's early winter trickle. The shining slit between the gray and barren banks smelled putrid, but the sky was bigger here, the river splitting the city open and traveling toward the horizon to places where she sometimes went on rural reporting assignments. Especially on days like this, she wanted to go away to parts of the plateau where the dry land stretched as far as the eye could see, where hill-size boulders perched on each other. She wanted to be there in a tent, living off air, bleached by the sun, a hardened survivor like the stunted trees. She remembered Raghav's old German Shepherd from when they were children and how Raghav had bolted from class and locked himself into the school toilet after the dog died. He would not be able to survive losing Chinna now. Since his heart attack five years ago, she spent the nights half-awake and if her sleeping husband did not move for a while, she crept toward him and laid her head against his chest to make sure she could hear life inside. The steady beat of his heart wound down her febrile watchfulness and let her sleep in snatches.

Muttering to herself, she started to walk again. Fuck the world, fuck the thugs who bludgeoned that man and savaged that woman, fuck the sodden suspicious vipers in it, fuck morality, high-mindedness. Her girls loved the dog. Raghav needed him. That was all that mattered.

Later that evening Elango smiled as he stroked Chinna's new collar. "Amma? When?"

"The one with the bells," Devika said, "it was frayed and dirty. I was passing a shop." Then she said after a defiant pause, "I've burned the old collar and leash. It's gone, his old life."

Dear Mrs. Vanamala Reddy,

I've always been puzzled by people who write to agony columns. I wondered how they could confide in a stranger, knowing their forbidden loves, ghastly diseases, and dilemmas would be published for the world to see. But here I am. I've been reading your column for years, and though I don't know who you are, I've come to feel a sense of kinship.

My husband and I were attacked on the highway. His right eye may never regain its sight. I merely have stitches on my head and a painful shoulder—everyone says I was lucky. They mean I got off lightly. But tell me, Mrs. Reddy, to whom can I say that I am badly hurt too? As soon as I shut my eyes to sleep, I see them. The hands all over my body. The things they said still make my skin crawl as if a colony of worms is oozing and seething on me.

And we lost our dog. I don't know where he is, alive or dead. If he has food or people who care for him. I published an advertisement, begged the police to find him, but so far there is no news.

My husband is still sedated a lot of the time and when he's awake I have been told to keep him calm. I have nobody to talk to. Is there anything you would suggest I do? (Please don't publish my letter.)

THREE

I

The seasons were shifting and the scent of woodsmoke hung in the air. Elango sat in his auto-rickshaw just outside the Moti Block tenements, luxuriating in the cool, too contented to move, thinking how time had a way of running through his fingers like water. The dog had come to him a year ago. So had his dream of a horse on fire, which had made him charge off to the pond to dig out the clay for it. That was all he had managed though the horse lived in his imagination, where it grew more statuesque every day. It was as if he was waiting for a sign to tell him the moment had come, the horse had begun pawing the ground, eyes hooded, waiting to be uncovered and led out to applause.

That sign arrived in the next few seconds. Through his curtains of half sleep he heard Zohra's voice.

"Free? Will you go to the post office?"

For a split second he didn't open his eyes, thinking her voice came from one of his daydreams. Then he shot up.

It was the first time she had spoken to him since the street market and he had visualized many scenarios for such an encounter. This had not been one of them. He was to have been carelessly stylish in his good shirt, hair combed, watch on his wrist. Instead he had been asleep. Had his mouth been open? Had he been snoring?

He scrambled out, giving her a quick, embarrassed smile. He hoped he had not left the back seat reeking of his sweat and took a few seconds to wipe it with a dust cloth before she climbed in. The auto-rickshaw was flooded with the scent of her—a mixture of soap and talcum, powdery and sweet. She leaned forward chattily while he cranked the lever to start the auto. "Other days, I walk. I didn't want to wake you, but I have to pick up my grandfather's pension and today I'm a bit late."

This close, her voice was smooth and warm. Like rum, he thought, sending out tendrils of heat and contentment into his deepest parts.

"I wasn't really sleeping," Elango said, sounding sheepish. They had exchanged no words for months, yet she was talking to him as though they were friends. He started the auto-rickshaw, began to weave his way through the crowded street up to the main road, then speeded up. She was a mere foot away. He could see her in the rearview mirror, eyes narrowed in the breeze, brushing strands of hair from her forehead as they came loose. A part of an eyebrow was interrupted by a scar and her collarbones jutted out from a neck as slender as the fruit on his moringa tree. In the bowl-shaped dip where her collarbones met was a blue pendant on a fine gold-colored chain. She looked away as soon as their eyes met in the mirror.

Never had a drive been more joyous. He went so fast on the bridge over the river, his neckcloth flew back like a flag. He heard her laughing, "I am scared! Slow down, I am not in *such* a hurry."

When women are in love, he told himself, they cry out to

the man to go slow, to stop. It was both a cry for rescue and a plea for captivity—in the movies it was always so. He looked over his shoulder and a thought passed between them—the same thought—he was sure of it. These things could not be mistaken. Why, of all the auto-rickshaws in the world, had she found his? He hardly ever waited for customers—he finished the school round and then went to work making pots until it was time to go back and fetch the girls. She had come out looking for transport at precisely the moment when he was dozing on the street. Dog. Woman. Horse. The same stars and planets had made it so. They had nudged her in his direction because of the fervor with which he had willed the universe to realign itself to make room for his desire. What he had to do now was to be patient, wait for the right moment, tell her his feelings with a prayer on his lips to the gods of clay.

For a start, he would insist on driving her wherever she needed to go—to the library where she worked, the post office, the ends of the earth. She said she needed only to go to the post office some days and to the dispensary in Kuttipally to get eye drops and medicines for her grandfather. They planned for Elango to wait a little way up the road whenever she needed to go anywhere and soon she was sliding into the auto-rickshaw as naturally as if it were her own. He took no money and she never offered. They had made no declarations or promises, but already some things did not need to be said between them.

2

Chinna had not lost his adolescent lankiness, but he was shaping up to be a big dog, chunky at the shoulder and paws, a little taller each month. Elango calculated his age as some months under a year and a half, if he had been about six months old when he was found. His tail had turned into a swaying banner, and his lopsided ears had flopped down into two triangles framing his head. He was known and loved in the neighborhood and people had their own special names for him. Elango's friend Giri claimed that his pet tortoise Hema Malini moved faster and always in Chinna's direction if she sensed him nearby.

The dog liked to escort people around or visit them at home. Elango was resigned to the fact that Chinna was given to going door to door and resting a while at each, until someone came out with a bite to eat. The dog never begged, he sat at the doorstep as if contemplating the world, serene in the certainty that he was irresistible. There was no need anymore for him to spend the mornings at Devika's, but he made his way there out of habit—not to mention the bowls of meat and rice. It was now one of the several homes on which he deigned to call during his daily rounds, and it was their privilege that he consented to sprawl under their fans. After a siesta, he padded about leaving no corner unsniffed as he passed the girls and their father, allowing himself to be petted by them, looking as if he was doing them a favor.

Evenings, Chinna waited at Moti Block for the blind calligrapher who lived there, Zohra's grandfather. The old man put out a hand with a courteous "Salam-aleikum, Miya" as soon as he reached the last of the stairs from his rooms above the shops. The dog pushed his nose into the hand. The man would tap his stick and set off with the dog for his constitutional. Later the calligrapher would say goodbye in formal tones, handing over a ghee-soaked roti that Zohra left in a particular place for the proper conclusion of their daily ritual.

Chinna's next stop was in the alleyways, to idle for a while, sniff around for females in heat, and growl at rivals. Then it was time to rest again, so he padded off in the direction of the pond. Elango was there a great deal these days. His submarine horse had come to him again during the night, wandering below the water of the pond as tongues of fire flowed from its nostrils. It was time for it to rise and shake the water off its mane and back.

3

Watching me making a pot one day, Elango said I had reached the stage for learning new techniques at the pond. He swore me to secrecy. "Not your sister or your mother or father or Lakshmi. Not your Fauzia either. Nobody must know."

I followed his directions, walking beyond the low houses and mud-and-thatch hovels of Kummarapet. Elango had told me not to stop at the first pond where pigs grazed the turd-strewn earth before their food dissolved in the rain. After that came an interminable stretch of scrub. Scratchy grass, mosquitoes. I scrambled through thorns, wondering if I was lost and should turn back. But then, passing a stand of tamarind trees, I saw the scrub and bushes open up—and there was the sky-filled expanse of the second pond, Elango's pond, with a leafless tree next to it, just as he had said.

The horse had to be made away from Vasu and Revathi, this was why he had to sculpt it by the pond. Elango explained no more. It seemed odd to me, for here he had no work shed. If it rained before the horse was fired it would be washed away, and to keep it safe during the time it took to make it, he had fashioned a lean-to with rusted tin sheets on bamboo poles. Next to the lean-to was the tree once struck by lightning. It wasn't much more than a scorched trunk whose jagged black top clawed at the sky, but that eerie wooden hand made the area around the pond appear utterly deserted. There was an egret gingerly crossing the pond, as if treading on glass, not water, and that was all. I looked around and it struck me how far I was from people, shops, home.

Elango seemed much taller than me beside that bare tree. He reached into it from one side that was partially covered by a creeper. "Look, I've got something here," he said, wild-haired, grinning. In place of eyes he had shining chips of moonstone. A thrill of danger rippled through me, as though I had been transported into one of the books I had read. Things happened to girls in those books that never happened to a girl like me, who had to go to school every day and at the end of term spew out chemistry formulas, draw the regulation *Hibiscus rosa-sinensis*, and rattle off "Daffodils" by William Wordsworth. None of that had taught me to understand the sensations rushing through me here by the gleaming water.

He drew out a watch. It was made of steel and had a broad band. He put it on and held out his wrist to show me. It was a strong, square wrist, and his hand looked big enough to hold three of mine.

"I found it in the forest where I found Chinna," he said. "It was just lying there, and he took me to it. It's his gift to me. I wear it when I work here."

I nodded, not taking in a word of what he was saying. He was in a singlet, stripped down to his shorts. The bare arm he held out toward me was long and sinewy, its muscles moved visibly with each gesture he made. I could not understand why, when he had looked this way since I was a toddler, I was suddenly self-conscious and shy.

The feeling passed once he set me tasks I had to finish in the next two hours. Every minute of my time was crammed with learning techniques, understanding processes, and during the few classes I had at that pond I came to know many things about Elango and his horse. Every year his grandfather and the other potters of their village had made a giant clay horse, modeling them here, next to the pond, close to the clay it would be made with and far from houses. That was when Kummarapet was still a village largely peopled with families who were potters by caste, still following their ancestral vocation. They had come as a clan from Tamil Nadu so long ago nobody remembered why or when. The area of our city now called Kummarapet had started as a village they established in Andhra Pradesh. One of the few things from the past they preserved was the tradition of making a clay horse every year—though that was gone now, along with the potters. The temple once held an annual festival in which such a horse was an indispensable element. Their gods wanted it as a sign of collective worship, it was ordained for reasons they did not know, they accepted it as a fact of life. It took several days to make and was then decorated and consecrated, paraded around the neighborhood with music and celebration. It was a divine horse, dedicated to the sons of Shiva, protector of the village. It shielded them from illness, bandits, evil. Remnants of those long-ago horses stood in the compound of one of the old temples even today, worn down by wind and rain. The potters who had made them were dead or gone and those that came after did not know how to make them.

The third time I went to the pond, I found Elango rolling a

ball of clay into a long and fat coil. "Pick up some clay from that mound," he said. "Get to work. Make a coil like this one."

He formed it into a circle, shaping a ring. Three more rings would follow, which he would position in the four corners of a rectangle he had drawn on the ground as a guide. These were to be the start of the horse: the legs. The legs would grow in height as new coils of clay were added to the original coil and then he would fashion the body, the head, the rest of it. When the horse was complete the work of making decorations for it would begin.

"That will be your job," he said.

The earth shaded by the lean-to was smooth and hard with years of use. I sat on my haunches to roll coils on it, thinking it would be easy, but I had to keep starting again as my attempts cracked at the edges or fell apart. After a while it felt pointless and tedious. I wanted to wade in the pond, flick flat stones into it to see how many times they would bounce before sinking. Elango seemed to divine what was on my mind and frowned at me. "Keep at it. Everything else can wait. Sprinkle a little water on the floor where you are working."

He put aside the coil he had been rolling and stepped into the pond. He started digging at the edge, knee-deep in sludge. He piled the earth he dug onto the bank and once he had collected enough, he laid his metal basin to one side and stepped into the wet clay. He walked around it slowly, in a circular motion, every now and then adding straw and rice husk from a mound that stood next to the sludge. He gestured at me. All at once, the strangeness of the first day came over me again—I was bashful and eager all at once and I also wanted to run back home, away from the confusion. Instead I walked tentatively into the clay he was working. My feet were immersed in it, then my ankles. If I slipped and fell, I would have to hold on to him, nothing else to be done.

"Stay where you are. Be careful," he said. "Sometimes there are glass shards or nails."

I had thought it would feel messy but instead it was silken and cool. It slid off my legs, it rose between my toes. I started to find my balance, move with more certainty. I was feeling my way around as he had shown me, slowly, when my feet touched something. I bent down to get it.

It was a disk of fired clay, broken on one side, and when I handed it to Elango he dipped it into his pail of water and wiped it on his shorts. The piece had a loop through which a string could pass. An amulet perhaps. A figure riding an animal was clumsily carved on it. We could not tell if it was man or woman, nor whether it was a horse or a tiger. A corner of the legs was where it had broken.

Elango had found other fragments near the pond before this, he said. He had a piece of a goddess's head, broken parts of pots, a horse's hoof, a few small dolls of the kind he still made for Diwali—he stashed them away in the hollow of the tree. It was continually miraculous to him that fired clay did not melt back to earth again—it could be broken or weather-beaten but it had a life force that was inextinguishable. "The pots you and I make," he said, "they may be around three hundred years from now. A thousand even." Each time he found something, he wondered if his grandfather or an ancestor infinitely more ancient had made it.

"Do you know that some people drown their idols of gods and goddesses in the river after festivals?" he said. He shook his head in puzzlement. All the way from Calcutta, giant clay images of Durga, Ganesh, Kartik were transported southward, where people would worship them as if divinely possessed, and after several days of frenzy, submerge the images in the river.

"I've seen it with my own eyes," he said. "Some are tearful, parting with the idols. But still they immerse them in the river—it's part of their rituals."

"Then why bother to make them?" I said. "It's just stupid."

"Not stupid . . . why do you think that? We can't always understand everything," he said. "I feel bad for the potters, though." He would sit there watching, wondering how those far-off potters, men like him, bore it year after year: their artistry surviving just five days. They did not fire those sculpted images in a kiln, and the potters who made them knew their clay would return to earth. Like dying every year.

We were sitting by the pond passing the clay amulet back and forth, talking, when we heard a rustle and an intake of breath. When we looked up, it was Zohra.

She was startled to find me there, I could tell. I didn't know that she too came to the pond; I had thought it something between Elango and me. He rose quickly to his feet, brushed his hands on his shorts.

"She's the student?" Zohra said. "Strange. A schoolgirl learning . . . here . . . what for?" She looked around at the pond, the lean-to, the mound of clay, and her eyes returned to my legs, muddy up to my knees.

"You need to wash those before you go home," she said.

Though she had turned away and was talking to Elango, I could not stop looking at her: the bronze skin of her face, miraculously smooth where mine had started breaking into spots;

the coral of her lipstick, which she must have put on just before coming; the scent of flowers that had arrived with her; the dark-eyed, mocking gaze she directed at me again. You could not imagine her with muddy hands or feet. For Elango and for me, clay was not dirt, I wanted to tell her. I didn't need her to tell me to wash my legs.

Elango moved aside too quickly, the amulet dropped from his hands to the ground. She drew away. "You dropped something," she said. "There . . . at your feet." She picked it up, observed that it was an amulet and she had just the string for it if he wanted to wear it. And also, she said, she needed to go to the central post office the next day and wondered if he would take her in his auto-rickshaw.

"Two o'clock?" he said.

"I'll be at the usual place."

That I had overheard their plan did not seem to bother her. She turned away without looking at me again and began a slow, wobbly walk back over the rough dirt path. Elango did not say another word. He appeared to have forgotten all about the lecture he had been giving me on the gods and goddesses of Calcutta and things potters passed down the generations. Instead he walked to the pond, as if in a daze, and picked up his spade, looking now and then at the path, as if he could still see Zohra there.

Something was changed. That invisible thing which surrounded men and women. I could not explain it, but there was the same fizzle in the air that accompanied every morning's prolonged goodbye at the door between the couple who had moved into the house opposite ours. After the man left, his wife Gauri spent all morning practicing romantic songs from the movies:

first we heard the original played on an LP, then her uncertain voice picking up a fragment of the tune. Late at night, after her husband was home and the rest of the quadrangle had fallen quiet, her voice would float across, as pinched and off-key as in the morning: *"Tum dur nazar aye, badi dur nazar aye . . ."*

I would lie awake mystified. Was this romance? On our recently acquired television set, a buxom actress in a bandage-tight sari approached her marital bed to the lilt of a languorous song. She held a huge glass of milk and as she handed it trembling and simpering to the mustachioed hero, something significant passed between them, and though it had no name I knew it as the thing I had sensed between Elango and Zohra. In school Fauzia and I had seen a boy waiting to pick up a girl from a different class. He would—he must—look at us. What would happen if he did? Who would get him, Fauzia or I? After some discussion we had agreed to share him, half and half. We did not think through the details of the arrangement. We were torn between him and Begum Tasneem's son, the only other young man on the horizon and therefore imbued with desirability. He left a trail of cigarette ash on the piano at which we would later congregate to practice "There Shall Be Showers of Blessings" for the school concert. Every girl in the class was more interested in showers of ash, secretly convinced the principal's son was leaving subtle messages on the piano keys.

It occurred to me that I had recently seen Elango immersed in a book while I was struggling through my coil-making. I couldn't make out the title because it was in Telugu, but the book had a painted picture on the cover of a man and woman, close together.

I was sure that for all the hours between the moment Zohra

left the pond and the next afternoon, Elango would think of nothing other than that she had walked the entire scrubby distance to the pond—despite her limp—to seek him out. It was more romantic than anything I had firsthand experience of. I needed to tell Fauzia as soon as I saw her.

4

On the day of the third India–Pakistan one-day international cricket match that November, my father took leave from work to listen to the commentary in peace. The frenzy of it came at us in snatches wherever we went—a radio was on at the shack near the school gates where we bought sweets and ice creams at lunchtime and one of the gardeners had it on next to him where he was at work. Periodically something on the radio made him exclaim, "Again! They've done it again!"

"Don't make excuses in advance," the gateman said. "Just because you're losing."

"Why don't you go and live in Pakistan if you're so keen on them?" The gardener settled on his haunches and lit a bidi with a lazy smile.

A green satin flag hung limp over the main gate of our school. It showed a lamp resting in the bowl of a crescent moon. On the signboard next to it, the name Safar was written in English and Urdu below the painting of an oil lamp of the kind Elango made hundreds of each Diwali. The school motto circled the lamp in a wreath made of long-limbed Urdu strokes. Begum Tasneem had set up classrooms in the stables and guest quarters of her family mansion. Alongside a maulvi to provide religious instruction to the Muslim girls, she added a sports teacher and running tracks, basketball hoops, swings, and jungle gyms to the lawns. A few of my friends arrived in burkas and in school they shrugged them off to reveal the same short tunics as the rest of us. Before leaving, they covered themselves again. Not everyone in the city could swim as easily between elements. The burkas, the flag, the Urdu, marked out our school as Islamic, and the gardener was not the only one suspicious of our gateman's loyalties.

When we went into our classroom after our tea break we found that a poster of Imran Khan had been sellotaped over the health science chart painstakingly made by Fauzia. He was a streak of lightning in cricketing whites, blazing against the green of the grass, captured at just the point when he was about to let a ball hurtle toward the batsman. The five of us who had entered the classroom gazed at him in mute adoration. A sixth, Manika, unpinned the poster and dropped it on the floor.

"That's where your Imran Khan belongs," she said.

"Oh, come on, Manika," Indu said, "we don't have to be supporting Pakistan, he's pinned up in our hearts."

"What have looks got to do with sports?" Fauzia said, and was immediately booed into silence.

Someone sighed, "*Hai* . . . When will they play here so I can shower him with roses?"

A quarrel ensued, both about looks and sporting abilities, and the matter ended with the usual mix of smirks and sulks until the early evening when we were out below the jaman tree practicing our lines for the school play. This year it was an abridged version of *Merchant of Venice* and we could make very little sense of Jewish moneylenders, Renaissance law, Italian aristocrats, not one of which we had ever encountered. As soon as the girl playing Antonio began, "In truth I know not why I am so sad," we would drown her out with loud groans. There were many distractions. Fauzia kept interrupting with her imitations of Babban Khan, whose play *Adrak ke Panje* she could rattle off to perfection in the local Urdu, leaving everyone teary-eyed with laughter. Apart from her, there were the sounds from assorted radios that grew more frantic and more high-pitched every hour. In a little while came the news that India had conceded the match to Pakistan without completing the overs. The captain, Bedi, had accused the Pakistanis of not playing fair. Sarfraz Nawaz was bowling "short balls" and the umpires were not doing a thing about it.

Within the hour came the news that a man had knifed another and a tea shack nearby had been set ablaze. Pig meat had been tossed into a mosque. The rumors spread like smoke from a burning building. In the northern corner of our playground was a stand of tall old trees from which fruit bats hung like moldering rags. These rags unhooked themselves from the trees and began dive-bombing through the upstairs rooms. We took cover under the tables, behind chairs. They never started moving before dusk and in the steadily sharpening panic, their erratic flights came as an omen.

The next part of it was swiftly blurred in my mind. I was told—by whom?—that we had to find a way to get home quickly because a Muslim school was an obvious target. I was rushed into a car by one of the burka-wearing girls in our class. She was from a wealthy Nawabi family and her car, its windows veiled with dark curtains, waited for her outside the gate all day. Fauzia was bundled in along with me and a few others. The car sped away, did a long roundabout route. I was dropped off last.

My father opened the door. "Home early? What's the matter?"

I gave him a breathless account of events. He barely paid me any attention. He was looking beyond me, outside the door, into the quadrangle.

"Where is Tia?"

His words dropped into the space between him and me like one of those bombs with a long slow fuse where you can see a small flame making its sputtering, reluctant way down a thread toward the explosives.

I had forgotten Tia. She must be in the junior school, waiting for me and for Elango's auto-rickshaw.

"You forgot your sister?" my father said. "You were in such a rush to run away you forgot your sister? What about your friends at St. Teresa's?"

We had no car. My father could look for a bus or auto-rickshaw, but he had no way of reaching our school quickly enough. He telephoned my mother at work and told her what had happened. I could hear her high-pitched anxiety escaping the receiver: "Why didn't Elango fetch them? Why is he late today of all days? *How could Sara forget?*"

That evening I sat at the table trying to pay attention to my mother's views on selfishness. Tia listened, eating her dinner with the expression of a particularly smug cat. She had not held back a single detail of how panic-stricken she had been, waiting for me in the junior school, expecting it every minute to go up in flames. She had told us about the gradual thinning out of girls as parent after parent arrived to collect their child. How all of them had offered to take her home yet she had been determined to await her loving sister. If I had been able to plug my ears or stuff her mouth with a cloth, I would have.

I went to my room and locked the door and through it came

the strains of the Beatles from our gramophone. I could hear Tia scream, "YALLOW submarine" when the refrain played, and each time I felt something twist inside me. I tried to turn my mind to the horse Elango and I were making, the submarine horse. That was the only kind of submarine I knew or needed, my private world of making pots was the one thing I would never have to share with Tia—or anyone else. I turned off the lights and held a pillow to my stomach to stop it cramping from hunger.

I sensed that the evening marked a change—an end and a beginning. An unarticulated hostility started to advance like slow-freezing ice through the flow of conversation and intimacy between Tia and me. It could flare up into bitter, angry quarrels, but most of the time we kept a distance from each other to pre-empt the spontaneity of even an argument. I knew instinctively that my childhood had been locked away that day and left at the barred gates of Tia's junior school.

5

Like every other Indian, Elango had forgotten the world beyond the cricket pitch the day of the match in Pakistan. Between listening to the commentary and throwing pots, time had slipped past him and he reached the school late to find both the girls gone, nobody knew where. It was only after two hours—gray with dread and driving—that he had come to know how the girls had made their way home.

After he had listened in silence to the caustic shower of words from the mother of the girls that evening, he retreated to the platform below a banyan tree in a half-dark street off Moti

Block. He could hear a childish song in the high voice of the stonemason's daughter and saw her perched nearby, playing by herself because nobody ever played with her. He ought to be kind, play with the child, but the off-key song in her breathy voice made him uneasy. He wanted to start his auto-rickshaw and go home yet his hands and feet wouldn't move. It happened to him sometimes that thick black ink flooded his veins where blood should be and a great weariness overtook him. When he sensed the ink's trickle begin, he did everything he could to dam it, flinging himself into work, but there were times when it swept in without warning.

As he was starting to feel he was drowning in black, Zohra appeared. Before he could fully register her presence, she was walking past him saying something.

"Come on—the other side of the road."

He left his spot below the tree and followed her at a discreet distance until they were away from the shops and tea shacks. When they had turned a corner into an unpeopled alley, she crossed toward him. His breath caught in his throat at the familiar scent of talcum and soap. She was very close, so close that the air felt as if it was not for breathing but something he could touch and feel, a wire strung taut between them.

"I had to walk back all the way from the library, there were no buses. The roads were empty," she said. "They said there was trouble. I thought it was the end. That I would never see you again."

She slipped her hand into his, pressing his arm against her side.

He held her hand tightly, knitting their fingers together. His own hand, calloused, strong and big-boned, felt enormous around her tiny, narrow-wristed one. His hands had broken heavy branches into two, lifted rocks, snapped the necks of chickens. He must be careful not to crush hers.

She did not let go of him until they reached the end of the alley and saw the shadows of other people crossing. She stepped away and walked faster even as he slowed down, so that when they emerged onto the main road she was several yards ahead, alone, bag strap firm in her hands, dupatta secure on her shoulders.

That evening, though Vasu and Revathi directed their customary barrage of words at him, though Akka butted in from over the wall and then made her widowed sister weep as on every night, Elango scarcely heard any of it. Each one of his five senses was far away, he had left them in that alley. He still saw and smelled Zohra, felt her hand in his, heard the soft urgency of her voice, tasted the instant when she had managed to touch her lips to his. He was struggling to comprehend what had happened, knowing only that it was bigger for him than the horse and Chinna and every other thing in his life.

The next morning, he woke feeling like a rainbow-hued bubble floating on a technicolor sea. He dredged and wedged hour after hour, his heart so light that the clay felt weightless. Back at the wheel, flowerpots and tea tumblers flew from his fingers onto the wooden board as if they were making themselves. He stacked the six giant urns ordered by Sudhakar for the Deccan Gold Hotel and drove the long distance to deliver them, the miles going effortlessly by to the rhythm of lovelorn songs he found himself warbling. When Sudhakar came down to the garden he found Elango in a reverie and, instead of examining the urns, broke into a smile. "Look at your face. Did you stumble upon Aladdin's cave? Tell me everything. Come on. Cigarette?"

Although he wanted to, he said nothing about it to Sudhakar over their shared cigarette. He tucked away the gift of a packet that his friend pressed on him and changed the subject. He would say nothing about it until Zohra gave him permission. The two of us together will decide about this, he told himself, rejoicing in the new sense of himself as one half of a pair. Within himself, he was elated by Sudhakar's question. It confirmed his sense of being transformed. He wanted it to be so. He marveled at the ease of it. Not a word had needed to be said—her hand slipped into his and that was that—and he was certain his mind would go back to that moment as long as there was breath in his body. It was a new way of being that seemed immediately familiar and yet electrifying. Breathtaking how swiftly she had asserted her ownership of him, how needless his fears or his rehearsals of the precise manner in which he would tell her of his feelings.

"Why didn't you say anything earlier?" she asked him soon after. "I waited and waited."

"I was afraid," he said after a pause so long she must have given up on an answer. "What do you see in me? I still don't know. It's the only time I thought I made a mistake not looking for a job after college . . . an office job. I could have been like Sudhakar, had an easier life. Everyone calls me wrongheaded to be making pots, driving an auto, earning a pittance . . . my father had such dreams for me. What kind of insanity is this, he'd keep saying . . . but I've always been obsessed with making things. And now you're landed with a dark-skinned fool who wades in mud all day."

"What do you see in a scrawny girl who's lame? But, Mashallah, you do," she said. They were talking in the parked auto-rickshaw at a distance from home and she put out a hand and brushed it against his arm when she could see that nobody was looking. The blue pendant in the hollow of her neck shone like a cat's eye. He longed to touch it but did not dare. It was still light and people could see into the auto-rickshaw. It was unbearable. He cranked the lever to begin the journey home.

He was getting used to her unfamiliar expressions, the alien idioms of her religion. *Tauba-tauba* was exclamatory outrage, real or pretended. *Mashallah*, she would exclaim in surprise or gratitude. *Inshallah* fell often from her lips, to express hope. Hope and amazement flooded him too. It was a continuous wonder for him to be owned, to have claims made upon him— he had never known anything of the kind. There was no little sister, his mother had died when he was a child. Before Chinna the dog, there was nobody who demanded his love or caresses or attention. She was far more reckless than he, and invented reasons to explain to her grandfather and a nosy aunt who lived nearby why she so often took an auto-rickshaw. On certain days Elango was taken aback by her need for him—the way her hands and lips found him in the darkness by the lightning tree—and she was willing to take a roundabout route to the pond so nobody would know where she was going.

If Chinna leaped into the auto when he was taking her, Zohra talked to the dog the entire distance as though the animal would understand every word. Elango loved her nonstop chatter. "See, that's the courthouse where my Abbajan tore his hair out trying to get back our home. Did he manage? Of course not—then we wouldn't live at that Moti Block dump. I would have a palace, and it would have a soft bed for you. That? That's a mosque. No, they won't let you in . . . mosques and temples aren't for naughty dogs."

And so on and on until they reached the post office, and she climbed awkwardly out of the auto-rickshaw and limped into the building, passbook in her hand, Chinna at her side. The dog would sit and wait for her by the mailbox outside the main door until she came back.

It was she who insisted they visit the exhibition grounds on the other side of town. An enormous fair took place there every winter. "Tell your brother some lies or just vanish and say nothing," she said, and he obeyed. They sped in the auto to the exhibition grounds as if airborne. They went from stall to stall, wonder-struck by the novelty of being out together after dark in this brightly lit place full of people who did not know them. The latest hit songs were playing on the loudspeakers, there was a sense of happy busyness about the place that lifted his heart, making him feel nothing was beyond his reach. Zohra shot at balloons. She won a plastic hen that laid a plastic egg if you pressed its sides. He bought her a hair clip. They found a dark spot behind one of the tents.

There was one stall for which you had to pay extra, the Daredevil Motorbikers from Marjana. He didn't want to go in, but Zohra had the money out before he could object. When you entered, it was as if you were gazing into a deep wooden well. The bikers went spiraling round the floor of the well faster and faster until they were riding on the walls at dizzying speeds. It was gravity-defying and unnerving, but Zohra cried that she wanted to ride the wall too, she wanted to fly down into the wooden well. When one of the riders tore off a helmet to reveal long, streaming black hair and flung away a jacket to uncover a sequined dress that rode over the curves of a woman's body, Zohra clutched Elango's arm and shouted into his ears, "*That's who I want to be . . . she's who I am inside!*"

Later, they drank sugarcane juice and ate fruit salad with toothpicks at a stall where they were demonstrating a new kind of grater that cut fruit in floral patterns. This was the grater she would have, she said, when they had their own kitchen.

Elango felt as if his heart had stopped beating for a long moment. Of course, he wanted to spend his life with her—but to hear that in words? So casually, as if it were inevitable? It wasn't. Zohra's aunt had started making caustic insinuations about her sudden need to go everywhere in an auto-rickshaw. Vasu and Revathi made sly jokes about pretty Muslim girls. It was still inconsequential, but in his experience, molehills didn't take long to become mountains. They would have to run away together. But where? And if he left Kummarapet how would he make pots again? Where would a big dog like Chinna live?

She never interrupted his list of worries. When he finished, she said this was not her way of thinking, and everything would fall into place, just as his shapeless masses of mud became beautiful pots. The facts of her life were now these: she had a job in a library that she would not give up, she had a blind grandfather to look after. She had Elango and Chinna. She had never planned to fall in love with a Hindu, but Allah had willed it so. It was not unknown for such a thing to happen and if men and women before them had found a way, she would as well.

Dear Mrs. Reddy,

I went back to the police station as you advised, and they more or less told me it was all my fault. What did I expect, they said, you stop on a lonely road in the dark and you wander in the forest though your husband has told you not to go far. I've realized they will do nothing to find my dog—they shrug and tell me to get another. Crimes become private sorrows as time leaches away their public significance, but surely they cannot go unpunished? My notion of justice is ancient. I believe in retribution. Anyone connected with my suffering will suffer.

My husband has told me we have to accept we have lost Tashi. But I cannot. Every day I mark a route on a city map and then take buses to different areas and start walking and searching. The other day I saw a young dog that looked just like Tashi. I called his name, but he was too far away. I've resolved to walk every street of this city till I find him. It may be pointless, but it keeps me sane.

FOUR

I

In summer I hated walking to Kummarapet. We woke from sleep drugged by the heat, and to leave our cool house felt like a trial by fire. I could see Tia lolling on the floor reading a book in deep shade, under a whirring fan. Elango's courtyard would be shimmering in the sun, and although his shed had a roof, it was no more than a tin sheet which became so hot that Revathi dried chilies on it. I stared at my father, hoping he would tell me I'd have heatstroke if I went out, but he did not look up from a table lamp he had taken apart and was trying to repair.

Across the backyard I could see Mrs. Khambatta in a sleeveless dress, watering plants. There was a long glass of something, probably cold, on the table on her veranda. She waved at me, sat down, and drank it all. Open-beaked birds hopped around me, giving themselves baths in a shallow bowl we kept filled with water. Outside our kitchen was a veranda with a washbasin to which our cook Lakshmi occasionally came out to douse her face and neck with water. She gave me a look of exasperation. "Still here?" she said. "Don't you have to go?"

Few people were around, even at Moti Block, and Chinna sat

in the shade by the steps, his tongue hanging out. His black coat shone, the markings on his face and trunk were a golden chestnut. When he saw me he thumped his tail just once or twice, as if nothing more could reasonably be expected from him in this heat, and at my call he rose with some reluctance. At Elango's house, Revathi gave the two of us a scowl in greeting and told me that my teacher had made himself scarce. "Make six cups, he has left orders."

Akka shouted from next door: "First the great artist breaks every caste rule and lets a girl use a wheel. And now he is too busy to teach her. You leave that mud and water, child, come and see what I've got here."

"My God, how some people have their ears against a wall . . . not a moment's peace!" Revathi yelled back. "Is it their business what happens in this house?"

The minute Revathi left the courtyard I climbed onto my stool and whispered over the wall, "Here I am. Quickly."

Akka reached up and handed me a laddu. It was golden yellow and crusted with raisins and cashew. She gave me a conspiratorial smile. "That will keep the little potter going many hours. Don't drop a morsel, it'll bring bad luck—someone brought them from Tirupati."

People were always bringing Akka gifts because they were afraid of her powers. Lakshmi even hid in the kitchen when she came calling. I wasn't afraid. I thought she was beautiful. Summer or winter, she was in silk saris and wore a diamond nose pin. Not a Saturday passed that she didn't walk around our neighborhood, face chalky with talcum powder, her black hair rolled up in an oil-slicked bun. She carried a small cane basket filled with rice grains over which were scattered flower petals and coins. A powdery stain of scarlet kumkum spread like dried blood over the rice. Her method was a combination of subtle threats and flattery. She got results by making rosy predictions about the future while implying they would only come true if more coins joined the ones on that bed of rice. Nobody knew the truth about her. People said she was warped because she had been abandoned by her husband and had no children; that she was cruel to the widowed sister who lived with her. My mother said women who earned for themselves and deferred to no one were universally disliked and feared.

Akka had always treated me as if I was something special for no reason I knew. When I was little and my friends made fun of my thin legs or snub nose, she would put her basket aside, sit down next to me on the steps leading up to our house, and wipe away my tears. Even today, I thought, she understood what suffering it was to sit alone making pots. It was clear to me that Elango didn't care at all.

I ate the sweet laddu she had given me, careful not to drop any of it. Then, after a long drink of water, I settled down with a ball of clay and a sulky face. This was not fun, it was an assignment. My absconding teacher had fashioned a cross out of two thin broomsticks as a gauge for the diameter and height of the cups and said he would measure them when he came back. This appeared to me the most outrageous high-handedness.

I sat on the stool before my new wheel, an object that demanded dedication because of the money and effort spent on it. I had not asked for one but seeing I couldn't handle alone the heavy floor-level one he used, Elango had designed an ingenious kick wheel for me. My father and he had made it together—measured, sawed, hammered, gone looking for ball bearings and a shaft. The usual weekend scene at our house was my father with some kind of machinery spread out around him. He repaired fans and plugs, he rigged up a home projector for us using a torch and a sheet of paper with a pinhole. He would be frowning and squinting through his black-framed glasses, a cigarette dangling from one side of his lips. Wreathed in its smoke, he would polish with linseed oil the wooden handle of a gun he had inherited from his father. He would dismember it and clean the muzzle and barrel, pushing in a metal tube covered with cloth doused in a potion he concocted. It was never used as a firearm. Maybe the gun had long forgotten it was a weapon and not an object of adoration. It had been put aside, however, for a new passion: the fashioning of my wheel.

What he and Elango had made for me had a small disk above, a bigger one below, the two joined by a metal shaft. I did not understand the mechanics of it but had to sit many times on a wooden stool while they adjusted the height until it was just right for me. Now, Elango's courtyard had two wheels: his big one at floor level, because he liked to sit on his haunches and throw pots, and a small one which I could kick and move on my own. All this time I had been making things with his help. Alone, I was lost. The ball of clay wouldn't stop wobbling, it became lopsided, the clay came away in dollops, it looked smaller and sadder than when I had started.

Elango was often away these days when I came on the weekends to learn. I did not know why. He seemed to be finishing his work at home early every morning and then disappearing. He had not asked me to come again to the pond after that evening when Zohra had found us there. Had she warned him off teaching me at that isolated place? *She must have!* I wrenched the soggy mass of clay off my wheel-head and slammed it into the water of the slop bucket beside me. The water splashed up to my face and beaded it with globules of mud. Why was I sitting here when I could be helping to make the horse, with Elango nearby, talking to me about his grandfather's workshop? Baffled resentment churned up my insides. I could not fathom my own anger—he had said from the start that he would not handhold me, I must learn for myself, put in the hours. The order and calm of his home shed was as always. His tools were laid out in straight washed lines, his clay was stored in vats that had existed in his grandfather's day. Nothing was different.

Or perhaps I had changed.

One hour later, soaked in sweat, I was down to my last ball of clay. I looked at Elango's urns drying by the shed, rows of identical pots and small teacups awaiting fire, each one given the spark of life by its creator, each distinct, perfect. Chinna regarded me with questioning eyes, as if troubled by my ineptitude. I thought maybe my clay did not want to be a cup—to be put into a fire and transformed. Perhaps it was turning into puddles in my hands because it would rather go back to the earth. Maybe every substance knew what it wanted to be, and my clay had doubts about becoming a cup even as I was experiencing strong misgivings about being a potter.

A fiery breath of air blew a shower of small dry leaves from the moringa tree onto my wet clay and a crow appeared in the courtyard, its beak wide open with thirst. Along with the crow came a butterfly, blue-black, huge-winged, so close I could feel it stir up air near my face. It dipped and floated, fluttered at a speed that made its wings evaporate as it hung suspended over my water bowl, then hovered above my face, my clay. I shut my eyes and felt it settle on my cheeks. Its feet moved across my face as weightless as a whisper. It reached my eyelids, then my forehead. It must have been a caterpillar on the moringa tree, I thought. It had found a safe haven and grown wings before the fire below the tree burned the rest of its tribe away.

When I opened my eyes, the butterfly was gone. The ball of clay looked exactly the same as it had a minute ago. I would try, but it did not matter if I made a cup or not. The clay would be what it wanted to be. I wet my hands. I kicked the wheel, faster and faster. This time, in a few minutes, I had a cup growing between my fingertips. Not flawless like Elango's, but unmistakably a cup.

On my way home I could not stop smiling. A caterpillar had escaped a fire and turned into a butterfly and my clay had become my first cup on a new wheel. Anything was possible. A baby mango was dangling from a wayside tree. I reached up and plucked it. Tart juice flooded my mouth. The theft made me happier still and as I passed the corner house where one branch of Taatha's family lived, I was humming a song. The widowed, silver-haired matriarch who lived there spent much of the day embroidering tiny sequins into pictures of gods and goddesses. She was always happy to put aside her needle and thread and chat with passersby. Today I could see Akka perched at her feet on the stairs by the grinding stones next to the kitchen. From a distance I could hear their voices rise and fall.

"What I told you last week is true," Akka was saying. "Something is up, I am never wrong about these things."

"What have you seen?"

"I've seen enough. The way the girl dresses these days . . . like she's off to join the movies. Three days running Ponamma said she saw her coming home late . . . where from?"

"What will you do?"

"Wait and watch. The time is coming. I'll know what to do . . . There will be a sign."

The old matriarch's spectacles glinted. I had trouble hearing what she said next, but I lingered to eavesdrop just outside their line of vision. She bent her head to her embroidery again and I heard her say, "Think how peaceful life would be if you had their house. Old women have a long memory. It should have been yours . . ."

"Don't I know that . . . a few months and they'll be slitting the throats of goats next door and drinking the blood. The potter comes home late. The girl comes home late. Can't we add two and two? Speak to Taatha. Plant a seed in his head."

"What are my powers or Taatha's before yours? You have a direct line to the supernatural! Still, let me see what I can do."

"And I'll do what I have to do as well," Akka said.

I did not know what she was planning, but she sounded utterly unlike the Akka who had been handing me sweets two hours ago. Her voice had an edge to it, as if she had dipped her tongue in venom before leaving her house with her alms basket. What had goat sacrifices to do with Elango? The image she had conjured up, of him slitting throats and drinking blood, made me shiver in the hot afternoon. I slid away before she spotted me there. She had always been kind to me, predicting that I would travel far and wide, become a great artist, marry a handsome man who would make me happy. But for those few minutes that afternoon it was as if she shed her kindness like dead skin, uncoiled herself, and hissed.

2

A few days later Elango saw Taatha walking around Kumma-rapet, muttering now and then, seeming to make mental notes. Where Taatha came, change followed. Heaps of sand or bricks arrived, land was dug up and new houses sprouted. Now he had paused to stare at the moringa tree. It was a pause so interminable that Elango stopped his work. Everyone knew that this house and its big courtyard had been a festering thorn in the old crock's side for years. He already owned much of the area and if all of it were his, he would have an uninterrupted swathe of land to redevelop. But the brothers refused to sell—in this one thing they were united—and their determination stood between Taatha and his grandiose real estate dreams. After a final ill-tempered look that he sent around with slow deliberation, the old man left.

"No hair, no teeth, no balls, but he's got his greed," Elango said to Chinna, once he had settled down again with his wooden paddle. He was going through a stack of half-dry pitchers, cradling them in his lap, between his legs, and tapping them with the paddle all over their leathery surfaces to round out their bases. His smooth, entirely spherical pitchers were in great demand in summer for storing and cooling water. The very last week he had supplied half a dozen to Taatha's household, and now he wished he had refused.

That same day Taatha paid a visit to Moti Block and raised everyone's rent. As consternation spread from one set of rooms to another, he stopped at the blind calligrapher's and looked into the cramped two rooms he rented him. The framed Urdu on the walls, a worn-out handbag slung from a hook on the door, a quill and inkstand on a desk, a calendar seven years out of date. The bed had a floral cover on which the calligrapher sat, awake after a recent nap, his white hair looking softer than wisps of smoke. His sleep had been too deep and he was still groggy from a bad dream, but he heard a creaking sound close to him and half rose, sensing an alien presence.

"Is anyone there?" the calligrapher called out, tilting his head to hear better. He heard footsteps receding and sat back on the bed, invaded by a sense of dread. He prayed his bad dream would not turn out a prophecy.

3

In the month of July we came home from school one day to find Lakshmi at the door. She spoke to Elango in Telugu, too volubly for Tia or me to follow, though seven mynahs stood in a row on the parapet next to our house, listening as if they could understand her. They moved sideways along the parapet for a better view. They scolded each other.

Elango turned to us and said, "Eat something quickly. I need to take you again." I recognized the tone: terse, abrupt, no room for chat—the one that came from people when things were bad.

This was my father's second heart attack. The first had struck at a time I could bring back only in shapes and splashes of color. A large doctor. Round spectacles. They came apart when he polished them too hard.

I had taken care of Tia that first time. She was four, and still called Tapti. I was seven, still called Sarayu. Another life. We sat in a big plastic tub used for washing clothes and splashed water on each other. We slept late and told each other stories in whispers. We did not understand that our father was expected to die. Apart from our having to be quiet, it was a life without rules so we could mash sugar into a cake of butter and eat it like pudding. But by the time I got to middle school, the weight of my father's illness pressed down on us at all times and the sense of his fragility settled within me so deeply that he seemed almost the walking dead, kept alive by twenty colorful pills every day. A pillbox with beads of sorbide nitrate clinked against coins and keys in his pocket at all times. Like my mother, we monitored his every ache and sigh. If he was late my mother started pacing about. What if he had toppled over somewhere like a tree in a storm? My father's heart was not merely a muscular organ inside his body. It was the fifth column in our house. Wherever we were, it was the beat of his failing heart that kept the time.

Speeding to the hospital in our crumpled school uniforms, dread started a slow crawl in my veins, as if a snail were creeping forward, trailing slime inside me. Maybe they weren't telling us everything, maybe it was much worse than Elango was letting on. He drove us almost all the way back to our school, then veered left toward an area of the city we did not know. The hospital looked like a museum, with pillars and arches and long windows. Three or four ambulances were parked outside, next to a set of shanties. I could smell dosas frying. A spurt of saliva filled my mouth. We trooped in past the red-and-white sign saying Emergency and came upon our mother sitting alone in the corridor—waiting for the cardiologist, she said. The chairs were metal. I counted the windows in the long corridor leading toward the Intensive Care Unit. Twelve, growing smaller as they receded. At the end of the corridor was the big door through which the doctor would at any minute come out. The windows were tall as in a church and one of the missing panes was papered over with a newspaper advertisement for tea that showed a woman in a bikini. Nurses walked past, preoccupied and impersonal. Not one of them looked at us. I thought maybe they did not know how to tell us that my father had died.

The week or so that my mother spent at the hospital, Lakshmi stayed nights in my room and one of my father's old camp beds was rigged up for Elango in the living room. This meant Chinna was with us constantly. The first morning when I woke to his wet nose pushing against my face, my arms reached out of their own accord and pulled him into my bed. We went back to sleep together, his scent sweeter than freshly baked cake, and for a while I forgot that my father was in the hospital. When my parents came back home, my mother pleaded with Elango to stay a couple of nights more—something might go wrong again, and she wanted him around. He appeared every night, bringing with him an alien smell of machine oil and clay. In the morning, well before I had woken up, he was gone. He reappeared barely in time to take us to school.

One evening I found—next to his camp bed—a thin towel, a steel tumbler for water, and a book I had seen him reading once before, with an amorous couple on the cover. Its edges were frayed now and when I picked it up it fell open to a page where the letter Z was etched in blue ballpoint all over: large, small, wreathed with flowers. He had made sketches on the blank pages at the back, all seemingly of the same woman: lying on her side or standing against a tree or pictured from behind by an arched window. I closed the book and returned it to its place, flushed with an unfamiliar, furtive excitement I did not understand. I ran to the bathroom, shut the door, and looked at my face in the mirror. Was it pretty? Of course not. Was anyone writing the letter S into a book somewhere for me? Not a chance, though the boy both Fauzia and I longed for had looked at me and smiled last week. I pulled up my T-shirt and inspected my chest. "Flat as the floor," Akka's voice said in my ears. "Give me twenty rupees and in a month, two at most, I promise you lotus buds." My mother had looked appalled, shut the door on her. I wished I had the twenty.

Contrary to my dark imaginings, my father recovered by degrees. Once the doctor said he could walk to the veranda, my mother insisted on paying Elango for the nights he had stayed. He resisted, but Amma forced an envelope into his hand. She asked if Chinna could stay with us a few more days. My father called for him first thing in the morning and said it was doing his heart good because the dog liked resting on his chest, being scratched on his back. They looked utterly at peace, sleeping together, she said, Chinna was the best possible heart medicine and her husband would be bereft without him.

4

The first evening Elango left for his own home without the dog, he realized it was he who was bereft. Though Chinna was a man about town now and wandered where he pleased all day, in the evenings he was invariably back. It felt necessary to have his dog within touching distance—Elango could not remember any other way of being now. Every evening Chinna came with him to the lightning tree. Elango lit his kerosene lamp, wound his wristwatch and put it on. The owl would hoot as darkness fell, and he would begin work, talking to the dog occasionally. Chinna did not reply but there was something about his presence that created a kind of music only the two of them could hear. Without him, Elango felt tired out. The making of the horse seemed futile.

Yet for weeks he had tried desperately to fit it in between his other work. He wondered if it was obtuse to carry on with it— hadn't it outlived its relevance? And after all the effort, might not a woman be mystified by the strangeness of being presented with a giant terracotta horse? Was it for Zohra that he was making it or for himself? It was hard to tell. The horse had become for him more an oracle than a clay sculpture and whatever happened to it would mean something. If it cracked open while it was being fired, it would be an omen presaging destruction. If he did not succeed in making it, it would signify failure, though he dared not spell out the kind of failure he now feared most— losing Zohra.

Evening was smudging away the outlines of the trees, making him feel as if he too were dissolving. When he couldn't quite see the ends of his limbs in the slow darkness, he had a curious sense of being disembodied and knew that if he did not get up, stamp his feet, light his lamp, he would be immobilized for hours. What saved him, as it often did, was the owl. It hooted and glided off to hunt. Back to work. Where was he? The legs. He was coiling clay for the legs.

Elango's grandfather had always consecrated the clay before he began work on a horse. He recalled sacred lamps, flowers, drums, coconuts, excitement. He had done none of that, reasoning that his horse was being made not as a god but as an offering for his own goddess. The horse was no longer a secret to her, but he had given her only the sketchiest account of his project.

On the day he lit the first bit of kindling for the firing he would explain it to Zohra, tell her how deeply it was intertwined with his love for her. He would fetch her when embers were all that remained and she would see the horse complete as it emerged from ashes. It would happen at night with no one nearby, only the black sky above, the horse glowing below, protected by no god other than the Dog Star in the heavens.

Who else would see it? One afternoon in a fit of cigarette-smoking garrulity he had blurted out his project to Sudhakar, watched him sit up with excitement. Elango was known for his tall, enormous urns. At the Delhi exhibition he had gone to, he had demonstrated the making of urns big enough to store grain, hold a human child. That was a stunt the photographers loved: a three-year-old with his head popping out from Elango's pot. This horse was his first large sculpture and Sudhakar was full of questions: how high, how heavy, how transportable. If the world had a lobby manager, it was Sudhakar. He looked at a plant not for its flowers or foliage—he would be assessing if it might fit in the arch by the desk. Urn or horse, he knew immediately where they could go, who would appreciate them most.

Elango relished his friend's excitement, yet was wary of it. The horse was a deeply private thing, inextricable in his mind from Zohra. It was the first thing he had ever made that served no utilitarian purpose, whose single reason for existence so far had been his need to give shape to a creature he had seen in a dream. He was beginning to wonder how foolishly romantic it was for him to be making this one massive thing which took up so much of his time but would bring in no money. Was it a luxury he could afford? But as he grew more certain about completing the horse, he was becoming aware of a new hunger in him, steadily more insistent, for it to bring him the recognition he now felt more confidently was his due.

That evening he fell into a reverie, thinking of the way his work would go into unknown hands a hundred years after him and at night he lay in the room he had built for himself, dreaming about where the horse might take him. Away from this stifling cell he had built for himself, with a few nails on the walls for clothes, a mat to sleep on. Away from Vasu and Revathi's newly minted barbs about Muslim girls.

Away with Zohra and Chinna.

He turned on his side, restless and aching. Most nights he slept under the moringa tree, Chinna and the stars for company. Without the dog, the courtyard felt empty and lifeless. The hens seemed to be searching for their tormentor.

Dear Mrs. Reddy,

You ask me to try and focus on other things. We are both architects, my husband and I. He's gone back to work, but I've resigned. I feel as if a bullet went through my brain and shot away my logic and focus on the evening I was attacked. I'm playing instead—I've laid out a scale model city in my guest room. It took days to make . . . I've added the tombs, the river, our well-known boulders. Here I am not attacked, my husband isn't struggling with his eyesight, my dog doesn't get lost, I am not in pieces. I can live.

Yesterday I walked all the way to Penda Hill. I went down every lane on the right side of Bharati Road and tomorrow I will do the left side. I counted fifteen stray dogs. Most were brown, two were black, one was white.

Tashi doesn't look like any of them.

It feels as if you are a friend. I wish I could meet you in person. Please tell me if that is possible.

FIVE

I

The blind calligrapher stood by Elango next to the lightning tree and ran his fingers over the legs of the horse. The potter had completed the legs and the trunk. Now he was determined to finish it before the rains came and washed his lean-to away. It would soon be time to start on the decorative work, and he had brought Zohra's grandfather there for a reason.

Elango knew his ideas might prove unworkable, but there was no easier way. He would have to inch toward completion by making a series of mistakes. Others might call it wasted time—not surprising, given that most people never made anything. How would they know about the fruitless, tiring days and months it took before your hands and heart and brain came together? Elango was close to that point, especially after an idea that had set him alight.

The blind man's fingers paused over the details of the horse's body, ran around bumps, stroked smooth surfaces, stopped again. His head was tilted to one side, as if he were hearing and sniffing his way to more information. Why only legs and trunk? Where was the horse's head, he wanted to know, and wouldn't there be a tail? What tool could he use on clay in place of a quill? He used to cut his own quills when he did professional calligraphy for books, newspapers, sacred sayings, wedding cards. People called him from far and wide—his strokes flowed straight from Persia, they said. He did not wish to disgrace himself with crude lines on clay. So what would be the tool?

Elango placed in the man's gnarled hands two carving tools, giving them a last look, reluctant to let go of them. The metal was shiny and sharp, the handles were made of polished redwood and had grips like no other tool Elango had held. They were from the set the Korean potter had sent him, and he had never used them for fear of wearing them away. Now their time had come. He had also set aside a few of the bowls awaiting the kiln for the old man to practice on, the clay of the bowls just damp enough to accept the impress of a knife or carving tool. He showed the calligrapher how to support the bowls from the inside when carving designs onto them, how to brush and blow away the clay that came off. The calligrapher peered at everything, crinkling his eyes as if he could squeeze sight from them, and settled down on a rock by the pond, wheezing out "Inshallah" every few minutes. He grinned into his white beard. "Old dog . . . new tricks . . . you have to keep me supplied with cool, clean drinking water. That's all I ask."

He was known as the blind calligrapher, but he was not entirely sightless. It was hard for him to convey what he saw on the days that he could see. Images floated by, distorted and fuzzy. Shapes and shadows loomed up, often too late to avoid collisions, and he had found out over the years that his streets were crowded with irascible men and women. At times great swarms of things he took to be flies fled past him and he swatted them only to find they were still there. He wore glasses but did not see well enough to know that one of the lenses had a fine crack and Zohra had not told him about it, thinking the old man needed humoring, not bad news. Whenever she could, she made him walk alongside her to the public library where she had inherited her father's job, shelving books. It was a building crusted with lime and plaster which descended in unexpected showers onto the books, but he liked sitting there, listening to the rustle of birds and pages.

Zohra had told Elango about her grandfather on a day when they had slipped away to look at the medieval tombs on the other side of the city. It was not that they were especially interested in long-gone kings, but the need to find somewhere to be alone together was now urgent and the possibilities few. After dark by the lightning tree their meetings were jittery and hurried, threatened by the arrival of someone who might know them. He wanted to be with Zohra as he had seen in the movies, out in the open, green and flowers all around.

She had raised an eyebrow and said, "Will I have to sing songs and dance around the trees?"

"I won't stop you," he said.

The tombs lay in a stretch of overgrown parkland across the river. Elango had seen them many times but only from far away. The biggest mausoleum was set apart and within its mildewed gloom were rows of stone coffin shapes speckled with pigeon shit, one so small he thought it must be the tomb of a baby. Around them was an undulating wilderness with trees and bushes and he saw that almost every bush was taken: men and women sat entwined in the privacy of leaves, some of them daring enough to be kissing. All at once he felt as if he were contracting into a shell. A great reluctance came over him at the stealth of it, at passion that had to be thus plotted and staged among skeletons in discolored tombs. It struck him as a travesty. There was a pang in his chest that made him turn away from the bushes—and yet, as soon as he could, he held Zohra's hand, put an arm around her waist.

"Don't, someone will see." She pushed his arm away.

"So what shall we do then?" he said. "Why did we come here?"

"To see the tombs. To talk in peace."

Talk? Stare at ruins? Were women off their heads? He stopped himself from saying those things out loud. At first they had been enchanting, the lovers' quarrels ritually followed by contrition and forgiveness. Not anymore. She seemed to view the world from an angle he often found incomprehensible and to his irritation she was able to outline her logic while he became tangled in his own arguments within seconds of embarking on them. He had no words, he only knew how to use his hands, he said. Could she not understand that some people expressed themselves with what they did, not what they said? She replied tartly that he did well enough with his mouth too, when words were not asked of it.

He walked ahead, feeling defeated. He looked at the moldy buildings, unimpressed except by the perfect curves of the domes and the symmetry of their arches. How had they managed it? It was hard to pull that off even with pots. Words in Persian were carved onto the walls of the tombs, loops, long strokes, dots, the script like a pattern that flowed across arches and down pillars. His annoyance was pushed aside by a thought. "Does your grandfather's calligraphy look like this?"

From that afternoon to this one: the calligrapher would carve Urdu words onto his clay. It would be a speaking horse.

The first touch of the carving tool on clay had made the blind calligrapher's hand tremble. He had not written anything for so long—could he do it now, and on this surface? The tool did not want to work with him—as he pushed it into the damp pot, its point hit fine pieces of grit or slid off the curve of the bowl. He ran his fingers over the letters he was carving and knew at once that they were crude, the work of an amateur. He rubbed at the surface of the bowl with a cloth and started again, feeling his way with his fingertips, longing for the familiar calm flatness of paper and the precision of his quill. Again the tool the potter had given him slipped, and this time it made a long scratch down the side of the bowl. He sat back on his haunches, lifting an edge of his lungi to wipe the sweat off his brow.

Elango looked up from his work. "It's clay and metal. It is not paper and ink." He held out his own mud-caked hands toward the other man and touched his arm. "These fingers have to find a different way to touch and press down."

He got up, wiped his hands on a cloth, and said, "Rest a little . . . it will take time. I'll bring you water and I have a little jaggery saved up. I'll tell you what my worry is—the clay must stay damp somehow, for many days, so you can carve on it. How do I manage that in this heat? I'll have to cover it all with wet cloth."

The calligrapher chewed on the small lump of jaggery, drank the water, then saw something white—it lifted off and went higher and his eyes followed it. Was it a bird or a piece of paper tossed by the wind? It turned into light and a shower of dark specks. All at once he said, "I know you're a good man and that matters more than your faith. But go far away with her if you want a future. Don't think about me."

He set his glass of water down and began to rub his spectacles with a corner of his kurta. "She is a good girl," he said. "I've been her father and mother since she was a small child. I'm happy she is making a life for herself—after all, how long will I be here for her?"

"What . . . ?" Elango was taken by surprise. "I want some carving on a horse. That is all. Who said anything about faith and all that?"

He regretted the words the moment they were uttered. Someday soon he would have to talk to the old man about Zohra. But then the man knew already, he knew too soon. If he did, others did too. There were many practicalities to think about and once all that began, nothing could be reversed. For a little while longer he wanted to hold on to his sense that their love was a jewel in a box to which they alone had the key. But this blind ancient she was stubbornly devoted to . . . It was a mistake to have introduced him to the horse. Now the man would start to advise him on everything, believing he had the right.

"I too am afraid of what is new," Elango said in a gentler voice. "Who isn't? You'll make beautiful carvings with a little practice."

"What will your people say when they see Urdu words on your Hindu horse? Have you thought of that? Isn't this a holy thing you're making for your temple? Your priests will not like it."

"It's not for a temple, nothing religious. Nobody from there will see it." Elango improvised swiftly: "A hotel has ordered it for their garden. I have to make it look good, that's all."

He turned away and there was a moment's silence, but then

he heard a snort of disbelief from the calligrapher. "Carvings for a hotel! What an idea! Hotels are vile places for vile people to do ungodly things. At this stage in my life," the old man said in a huff, "I don't want to insult the flow and beauty of the script I have always revered. My work has meaning."

"And my work has no meaning? Didn't they carve your script into stone on those tombs? You think clay doesn't match up to stone?"

Elango did not often lose his temper. Quite apart from the calligrapher's age, which demanded respect, Zohra's grandfather was the last man he could afford to offend. Yet now that he could see in his mind's eye his terracotta horse with beautiful Arabic script all over it, any other kind of decoration would be a compromise. It made him feel he would explode with anger: at his own pitiable workmanship, this calligrapher's obdurate demand for perfection, his dwindling supply of clay. He did not say another word but was aware of a crackle around himself, as if he were not a man but a high-tension wire.

The calligrapher, sensing his annoyance, got up with much groaning, dusted his lungi down, and said he was off for his prayers. Elango stuck his spade into the pond's bed and said in a savage undertone, "Yes, yes, keep praying. What else is there in life?"

2

In the main street near Moti Block, Akka stood waiting at Sharma-ji's grocery store for his weekly donation of five rupees and saw the blind calligrapher tap his way down the street. He was coming from the direction of the pond. She observed the old man's progress with an impassive gaze, secure in the knowledge that she could stare without being noticed.

"Do you need any help?" she said in a cooing voice as he came closer. "Where is it you went? You look so hot!"

"Ah . . . just that way . . . it is nothing."

"That way? Into the wilderness? Where?"

"Oh, you know, I felt like a walk. Hadn't seen that side for so long."

"The pond? You went all that way?"

"Oh no, not to the pond," the old man stammered, at a loss for a quick lie. He shuffled away, tapping his stick, before she could ask another question.

"But there is nothing else in that direction . . ." she called after him, then turned to Sharma-ji, rolling her eyes. "Who does he think he's fooling, that senile mole?"

Sharma-ji laughed as he fished out five rupees for her basket. "He went to see the future son-in-law at work, yes or no? Get ready for some beef-eating next door, Akka, and prayers five times a day. The mullahs are on their way to your neighborhood."

3

Kneeling and rising and kneeling again at his prayers that day, the calligrapher found himself straying from thoughts of God. He could still feel the tool touching the surface of the bowl, the letters starting to appear. As his sight had dwindled, his work had become worse, then stopped altogether—what use was a blind calligrapher? His fingers had forgotten how it was to hold his bamboo quill or hear its sound on paper—inaudible to all but himself—to see the strokes appear one by one, forming pages of beauty and learning. Carving those letters on the half-dry pots, it had seemed miraculous that he did not have to see what he was writing—his fingers could tell. He had been excited and afraid all at once. Afraid of failure . . . That sensation felt almost novel today though he had been used to it at the start of all difficult work.

The next afternoon he put on a clean kurta, discarded his lungi for a pair of narrow pajamas, placed his skullcap on his head, picked up his stick, and was out of the door, down the dingy steps of Moti Block and into the street before he could be stopped by too much thought. Raju at the tea shop called out to him to ask where he was off to in such a hurry, did he have a train to catch, and did Zohra know he was going? The calligrapher merely raised his stick in reply. When he brought his hand down again, it encountered a soft dampness. "Miya?" he said, and smiled into his beard as he stroked the flat of Chinna's furry head. He fondled the velvety ears and scratched him on the neck. Then he said, "Shall we start?"

This part of the lane, where he and Chinna were a familiar sight, was easily done. People moved out of his way and he knew every lamp post, rubbish heap, jutting ledge, and sharp corner. He kept to the side, but not too much because he knew from experience that open drains were slimy nightmares you could easily trip into. At the top of the road he had to change direction and walk south. When he felt a slap of hot air from a speeding bus he knew the intersection had come.

The main road went toward the big school and eventually to the old city where the alleys were a labyrinth of shops for cloth, grain, metalwork, biryani. Pearls that were sold by weight like rice or dal. He had not been there for years and did not need to worry about that, his destination came much before and his feet would remember and find their way. There weren't too many turns and it was on the riverbank. "It's not very far," he told Chinna with a tremor of uncertainty in his voice. "Just stay with me."

The way some hearts might race at the thought of reaching a lover's home, his breath quickened as he drew closer to the building he was walking toward, a mansion turned into an archive for Urdu books and periodicals. He knew the treasures on its shelves and in its basement vaults. His working life had been spent there, copying documents, imitating the beautiful strokes in some old parchment. There had once been a table and chair for him in there—they called it Usman Bhai's throne—with a strong lamp, a reading lectern for heavy books, and space for him to spread out his paper and ink pot and the quills he shaped for himself. The process was slow and laborious. He had to set his habitual impatience aside, knowing the bamboo needed to be cut and trimmed to achieve by careful degrees the sharp, angled edge he needed. Once he was satisfied with his quills he would dab a little blob of ink on his left thumbnail. Before the first stroke of the day he would murmur the name of God and then the strokes would flow, sure and long and perfectly balanced. On the days there was no calligraphic work to do, he read—he still remembered lines from the poems of Ghalib and Rumi. His feet now walked to their rhythm. But even as his lips murmured the magic words, he collided into someone—a man who asked him in an angry shout if he had buttons for eyes.

He heard a low, menacing growl from Chinna and felt the dog's warm body closer by his side. The voice of the man shouting at him grew louder before it receded and the calligrapher stood still for a few moments, then found the stick he had dropped. He stroked Chinna and said, "Miya, today you will get not one roti but two, and a kabab." He started walking again. He must not allow his mind to wander. Where was he? He had gone straight after that turn, and now there were no turns before the river. His nose would tell him when he reached the river: the water smelled foul these days, a blend of rotting sewage and offal and chemicals that made you gag. In his childhood—he often told Zohra this—the river was so clean its water was sweet enough to drink and swim in. How the trees bent down over the banks of his childhood and . . . Again his mind wandered—again he felt an impact.

This person was gentler. "If you can't see properly, at least tie your dog and hold on to him." The man's shadow was bulky and tall and it reached toward him and steered him to one side. At length, after a few more bumps and several near misses, the calligrapher reached the archive. He stopped at the door and touched the dog on his neck. "Miya, you seat yourself here and wait for me. They won't let you in." He waited until he felt the dog settle down by the door and then asked someone to lead him to the desk and said, "Adaab. I have a humble request. I wish to read the pages from the *Baburnama* you have here." With a burst of old pride he added, "I am Usman Alam, the calligrapher who made those pages. It was forty years ago."

The youth at the desk said, "Dadaji, you can't see your way to the desk, how will you read the *Baburnama*? Besides, we have hand-copied pages nobody is allowed to see without permission. Give an application today, come back for it tomorrow."

The calligrapher leaned wearily on the counter. What lunacy

had made him half kill himself coming this distance and how would he find his way back?

Even when his vision had begun to fade, he had kept working, a feat he managed by balancing two opposite ideas in his head: accepting in the abstract that he could become blind and helpless and at the same time telling himself he would not. The whole of life, he thought, is a matter of knowing the worst might happen and yet carrying on as if it will never happen to you. Had he ever thought he would live to bury his wife, his son, his daughter-in-law—the last two of them within days of each other, killed by fanatics in a riot in which little Zohra had been made lame for life? How the child's thin, soft leg had dangled in his arms, the foot swinging like a pendulum when he was running with her down the back lane. If only Zohra had come here with him—but she was too busy. Nowadays she was always too busy.

The calligrapher's throat had an unexpected lump, he could not swallow it. He should go out and sit at the door next to Chinna. He was thirsty, his legs were cramping, he felt himself yawning although he wasn't sleepy. This had happened to him before a blackout last year. He had to go back home somehow. He was steeling himself to grope his way out when he heard a voice from inside the offices that sounded familiar. It was calling his name in tones of surprised delight. It came closer and then it offered water, tea, a chair. The voice said it had been his student long ago and learned his calligraphy from him, didn't he remember Sadiq—the Sadiq whom he had scolded as a shirker? He could not place him? No matter. The man took the calligrapher to his desk, saying with pride that it was now his, but he would happily forsake it for the time it took his teacher to find the books he needed.

"What did you want to read? Tell me, I will get the books."

"I can't read any longer, son," Usman Alam said. "But something happened . . . it made me hungry for words again. I wanted to smell and touch the books. I wanted to hold them."

He felt his own hyperbole overcome him and his head sank to his chin in confusion. He patted the seat next to him. "Could it be that you, my young friend, will have a moment or two spare to sit a while and read for me? My eyes will picture the words from memory."

4

Elango completed his horse at the end of that summer. It was more than a year and a half after he had begun thinking about it. Twice in the past fortnight his brother had come to the lightning tree, bristling with questions which he had fended off saying he was making the horse to sell. He persuaded his brother that Sudhakar had promised a high price for it, and that if this first horse satisfied the Deccan Gold's owners they would order more for their other hotels. He felt himself breathe normally only when Vasu nodded, swallowing the story, though the swine aimed a kick at Chinna as he left.

Even after the horse was all but finished, Elango had to wait out the few days left of the month of Ramzan—the calligrapher could not work in the heat when he was fasting waterless. In the darkness before dawn, he heard the sharp, high voice of a man who walked through the lanes waking Muslims to eat their morning meal before sunrise. He thought of Zohra, foodless, waterless, and the many alien aspects of her life. He knew very little about the fasting and the subsequent feasting though he lived alongside Muslims in the neighborhood. Their lives were sealed off from his. He wondered about the little girl Fauzia, whom he took to school. Was she fasting? Did they do this to their children too?

"Will our children have to fast?" he demanded of Zohra.

She had fasted when she was a child, she said, and she still did. She drank water like a camel before the siren went off at the mosque at four, telling them to stop eating and drinking. It gave her headaches and made her dizzy.

Elango counted off the sirens. Each day that the sirens fell quiet brought him closer to the time the horse would be done. Finally, the business of Eid over, the blind calligrapher got to work. The potter had borrowed two wooden stools from the tea shop for himself and the old man to stand on to reach its flanks and withers. The calligrapher could not work for long stretches, his arms grew tired and his fingers started to lose control. It was a struggle to keep the clay damp in the heat and Elango had to keep bringing pails of water from the pond to sprinkle onto the horse, which he then covered with damp cloth, water-soaked newspaper sheets, and a tarpaulin he had salvaged. Every day he opened only the part the calligrapher would be working on. He had given up the idea of elaborate carvings, nor asked anymore what the words in Urdu said. The calligrapher told him they were lines by a famous poet and that was enough.

The script looked delicate yet strong climbing up the horse's sides from the fetlocks, which the calligrapher had carved lying flat on the ground. It ran up to the elbows, covered the back and loins, came down the forehead with a flourish to the muzzle. The calligrapher made a stroke, felt the indentation with his fingertip, then carried on with the next, oblivious of Elango watching him from a distance in silence, still puzzling out why the calligrapher had come back to him radiant with confidence only a day or two after he had walked off.

"From what well did you go and drink a magic potion, old man?" he asked the calligrapher, who cackled raucously and said, "The well of memories, Elango, the one you are not yet deep enough to have."

"And what text did you decide to carve?" Elango asked him in a cautious tone. They had had words over this. Usman Alam had scoffed at the potter's view that Zohra's name could be carved all over the horse, and given him a sermon on the glories of literature.

"Is it a poem?" Elango ventured again, getting no answer.

"You will know in time," the calligrapher said. "I thought of Ghalib . . . but then I had a better idea. You will see. Don't disturb me now."

It was as if the calligrapher had transferred the certainty of sight to his hands, which moved without hesitation over the surface of the horse, stroking and carving lines that followed its curves and hollows. His round knuckles were as shiny as berries and his dry, brown skin was like the bark of an ancient tree. Elango turned over his own hands to examine them as if he had never seen them before. He gazed at his rough palms and the yellow fingernails crusted with clay. To think these chunky things joined to his wrists spun out kilos of clay into huge pots and made the long, narrow necks of pitchers, Zohra had said, placing one of his hands on her own neck. Such gentleness, such control, she had said, looking at him through her eyelashes in the teasing way she sometimes had. She had held his other hand

and stroked the lines on it—too many lines, like the maze of a brain imprinted on a palm, she said. It showed a complicated mind. A dangerous one, he had growled.

At the end of a week's unceasing work, Usman Alam said it was done. He climbed off the stool, put down his tools, and was about to lower himself to sit with a sigh when Elango told him to go home and rest, and send Zohra with a little food and water for him. That was how it was with the young, the calligrapher grumbled to himself on his way back, they have no time for you the minute the work is done. They use you and then don't spare five minutes for pleasantries and gratitude. In his day . . . but when he tried holding back Zohra to tell her how it had been in his day, she too left, saying over her shoulder, "I'll come back soon. I've left food and tea for you on the table."

It was half-dark by the time she reached the pond by the roundabout route she took. Elango could hear soft exclamations as she twisted her ankle or stepped awkwardly. Maybe she could hear his heart beat, it was the thud of a drum. He had shelved thoughts of showing the horse to Zohra only after it was finished—what if it broke into a hundred pieces with the heat? You never knew what happened when fire touched earth.

Besides, he had a plan.

When she arrived he asked her to put down the food she had brought. He stood close to her and trailed a finger down the length of her spine. She shivered. Closer, he said, and she refused because he was smelling of earth and sweat. He told her irritably, because they had gone through this before, to get used to it. She was going to marry a potter—that was how he would always smell.

He went to the tree and took matches out from its hollow,

pumped and lit the kerosene lamp. She shielded her eyes against its harsh glare.

"Are you off your head? That light can be seen from far away," she said.

"They are used to it. I work here every evening."

He pulled her to one side and told her to shut her eyes. He stepped away, took the tarpaulin and sheets off the horse, asked her to look. He followed her gaze. To his surprise, seeing it with her eyes, the eyes of one who had not glimpsed his dreams or the animal's reality, he saw it did not look like a mule or donkey or a mean lump of earth. It had grown into the stately horse of his long-ago dream, the kind he remembered his grandfather making all those years ago. He saw her lips come apart, heard the sharp intake of her breath, and then her hands were all over the horse and she walked around it, holding the lamp closer, murmuring the words her grandfather had carved on it.

> Listen carefully,
> Neither the Vedas
> Nor the Qur'an
> Will teach you this:
> Put the bit in its mouth,
> The saddle on its back,
> Your foot in the stirrup,
> And ride your wild runaway mind
> All the way to heaven.

He had applied a wash of black slip before the calligrapher had carved the words. The carvings were the original khaki of the clay, the rest was the black of the slip. The khaki would turn terracotta red when fired, the body would remain black, he told Zohra. But first he needed her to do something.

He handed her the carving tool and said, "I've left space there—see? Now I'll hold the light and you carve our names—yours, mine, and Chinna's—into the horse. In your language."

She steadied her hands and carved their three names into the horse. At the end of it she looked at her work and flung the tool down, annoyed. Her letters were clumsy and cramped next to her grandfather's elegant strokes. But there was an intimacy to their homeliness that made Elango stand behind her, rest his chin on her shoulder, and tell her the script was not as beautiful as she was, but it was as precious.

She rolled her eyes and said, "All this sweet talk now. We'll see a few months after we're married, you'll be yelling at me like the rest of them."

5

"How is it I don't see the little one at the potter's these days? Has she stopped learning from him?"

My mother never had much time for Akka and rarely met her, usually being at work when she came around. She dropped a few coins into her basket and retreated from the door.

"I think he is busy," she said. "They'll start again when it is cooler." She turned away and went back in.

Standing on our veranda, Akka spotted me nearby, going off to Fauzia's, and asked me to stop. She came carefully down our stairs, balancing her basket against her hip. She was in a sari as blazing yellow as the sun and her skin shone in its glow. The smudged bindi on her forehead stared at me like a third eye. I remembered the day I had overheard her plotting Elango's downfall and felt a twinge of unease. She wiped the sweat off her face with a corner of her sari, held out a sweet laddu to me. "Have that," she said. "I know you like it."

I took a reluctant bite from it, knowing sweets broke me out in more spots, not daring to turn it down. She stood observing me. Then, as if she had made up her mind about something, she said, "Why don't you come to our side these days? It was nice to talk to you over the wall."

I mumbled, my mouth filled with the sweetness of the laddu. "I'll come again after some days. He is busy."

"Busy? Busier than usual? Why?"

"He is making something else. Something big. He has too much work."

"Ah . . . the poor boy . . . he has no help. I feel sorry for him. When he was little he used to be with me the whole day. His mother never had time to look after him . . . he is like the son I never had. I wish he wouldn't work so hard in the heat. Where is he working, if not at home?"

"At the pond."

"Have you been to the pond?"

It was an idle question that slid out as she adjusted the pleats on her sari with one hand, fiddled with the rice and coins in her basket. Before I knew it, I had shrugged and said, "Oh yes, of course. I wander about everywhere." Then, too late for retraction, ". . . I didn't go all the way to the pond, but I wanted to see so I went a little way. With the dog."

"You are lying, little one, I can tell."

Her voice made me stop munching and edge away. She made

a soft kissing sound with her mouth and said, "Ahaa . . . come, come. I've blessed and kept my Sara well all her life. If I am to keep you safe, I need to know where you are."

"I went there only once or twice . . ."

The dust of the quadrangle felt as if it would rise and suffocate me. I wished someone would call me and interrupt this conversation, but the houses were curtained off against the fierce heat, and the usual weekend vendors of fish and vegetables had not yet come. Even Gauri's husband, who had been outside washing his car, was gone.

She must have noticed the fear in my eyes because she mustered a kindly smile and lightly touched my cheek. "You're my favorite child, aren't you? And you wouldn't lie to me and hurt my feelings. Now tell me, did you see anyone else at the pond? Apart from Elango?"

I thought of Zohra reaching out for the amulet, I thought of the look that had passed between them, of the sketch of a woman I had seen in his book, the letter Z he had written and adorned over and over again. I thought how Elango had given me very little time after she had entered his life. "There was only one person, a lady . . ."

"What are you muttering, child? Did you say something?"

"Only the dog," I said loudly, looking straight at Akka with innocent eyes. "Elango-anna wanted to teach me something so he called me there."

She appeared all of a sudden to lose interest in me and hoisted her basket securely at her waist. "Look at me, standing here and rattling on when I have a hundred things to do. You run off where you were going."

She began to walk down the lane toward the house where

Taatha's relative lived. But after just a few steps, she turned to me again.

"What is this big thing he is making? I could go across there and see it anytime, couldn't I?"

"It isn't made yet. I haven't seen it."

"But what is it? A god or goddess for the temple?"

He had told me to say nothing about the horse. However hard Akka's eyes bore into me, I would not say a word. I think I was stammering when I spoke.

"I don't know. I only prepared some of the clay."

This time she turned and walked off more decisively toward the next house and as soon as she was gone, I broke into a run in the direction of Fauzia's and kept going until I was there. I called her name at her gate, panting hard. We never rang each other's doorbells, always preferring to shout and wait outside. *Why was she taking forever to open her door?* Though I had said nothing about Zohra, if I went back over the conversation, I could no longer decide if I had given away too much or nothing at all. I needed Fauzia to tell me I had done nothing wrong. That everyone knew Elango worked at the pond, that he was busy, that if I said he was making something big, it didn't matter. We retreated to a niche by the house down the road and settled on the steps leading up to a small latched gate where we could not be overheard. Fauzia agreed I hadn't said anything Akka could not find out for herself. The pond did not belong to Elango, other people could go there—even though they had no reason to. And if she knew he was making something big, so what? He made all kinds of things.

Once we had dissected the matter and every part had been examined, we began to flip through the pages of the latest

Sportsworld. "RIP Indian Cricket," said the black-banded cover, followed by paragraphs of anguish from Pataudi. A few pages inside was a story on our latest hero, John McEnroe. Our absorption was immediate and intense, and questions of guilt and culpability were wiped clean from our minds.

Dear Mrs. Vanamala Reddy,

No, time does not heal. Let me tell you some wounds never heal. Have you ever had such a wound? It gnaws you hollow from inside like termites deep in the leg of a chair, which collapses when you sit on it though it looked whole and new. The termites are at my skull, Mrs. Reddy, some nights I wake up and my pillow is gritty with powdered bone. But they haven't got to my brain and I won't let them. I am flint inside. If you split me into two and strike one of my pieces against the other there will be sparks. You will breathe the scent of burning stone.

Today I did Basuri Nagar, Model Colony: they have all the ugliness of modern architecture and none of the comforts. I notice brown dogs dominate the streets. They come to me like old friends, they know I won't do any harm. I will never give up looking for my Tashi. You can be sure of that.

SIX

I

When the horse had dried thoroughly Elango dug into his patiently collected stash of wood and brush and the dung cakes he bought from the buffalo keeper. He arranged the dung cakes first, all around the horse. He carried on methodically: dung cakes, then the wood he had brought back from the forest, topped with old fired pots. He stacked his other unfired pots, pitchers, and cups under the horse's trunk. Remember to pile in dung cakes there, below the trunk, he told himself. Remember once you are done to sweep away everything else that might catch fire. However many times he fired pots, there were things he reminded himself to do.

More dung cakes, more wood, more old fired pots until he had reached the end of the horse's neck and then he heaped straw on the pyramid he had created. After he finished you could not see a horse, it was hidden under what looked like a haystack. He paused for a break, had a quick smoke and a swig of water. Chewed on a piece of jaggery and threw Chinna one of the idlis he had brought with him.

He had mixed buckets of clay slurry to lather the straw with.

This was the most tedious part, one he always disliked doing though he had to for every firing, and he got down to it, humming a monotonous melody that had been stuck in his head for days. It was a song about how everyone came into the world crying and only a few left it smiling. Those were destiny's victors. Repeating the same lines like a chant, he slapped the wet slurry onto the straw, bending and straightening without pause as if he had been transformed into a machine that knew no fatigue.

He was nearing the end when he heard the owl hoot, as if asking him how it was going. He realized darkness was falling fast and was grateful for the companionship of the owl, the thought that the work was almost done. He would eat a big meal today. Not at home. He would buy a plate of Raju's goat meat, succulent chunks he probably cooked up with engine oil and chili paste. The oil floated on top of the fire-red broth, bearing slivers of curry leaves. With that there would be a big bowl of soft, plump rice. The thought made his mouth water as he worked. "We deserve a feast, don't we, Chinna?" he said to the dog, who was snapping at flies nearby. "Our stomachs can't fill with just insects and pond water."

He laid clay slurry on the top, leaving the usual opening, and at that instant was reminded of his dream. The dream of a great horse on fire from which he had woken panic-stricken that he had not left an outlet for the heat and gases. That day had led to this one and yet it felt as if it was from another life, like all the years that had gone before Chinna and Zohra.

After the horse was entirely covered and he had cleaned up, he lit a torch and circled the mound, touching it along the base. Small tongues of flame appeared. Once several fires were burning at the edges, Elango threw his torch into the fire as well. Tendrils of smoke thickened and rolled out from the mound. He had given up thoughts of goat meat and instead spread a lungi on the ground and lay down by the pond with Chinna. His body glistened with heat and sweat and he fell into the sleep of the exhausted who could make a pillow of a stone and not stir or dream.

Flames woke him up—the sound of them, the glow of them. The mound was blazing. He sat holding Chinna safely away from it, looking at the orange flames in the black night. The dog trembled in his arms and he murmured calming nonsense to him, but as a piece of wood crashed and parts of the mound fell, Chinna began to pant. Elango shook him by the fur at his neck and told him not to be a sissy.

By morning, the fire had gone down but the blackened heap of straw and clay was still smoking. He decided he needed to cool off so he stripped and waded into the water, sighing as the heat of the night was washed away. Chinna jumped in too, ears flying backwards, and paddled toward him, tongue out, mouth wide open. Elango threw a stone for him and the dog barked as he swam away after it. "Look, Chinna," Elango cried out, pointing at the cloud-heavy sky. "We finished the firing just in time. The monsoon is on its way."

In a while some of the hardened clay slurry fell off the firing mound and revealed the head of the horse. The ashes started to cool. Toward evening, when Elango came back to the pond, the rain began, and as it washed away the straw and ashes, the horse revealed itself, a smoky black and red. The potter stood for a long while, wordless from the wonderment of seeing his creation in its final form. Had he really made it? Could any human being have made it? Rearing out from the ashes, its eyes staring straight ahead as if they could see things beyond the earthly, the horse he had made seemed to him to be a divine being. He bowed his head to it as if it were a god, sent it a whispered prayer of gratitude for arriving intact on earth. He left only after the darkness had shrouded it.

Rain fell steadily through the evening and night. Elango lay in his rough shelter at home listening to the hard patter on the tin roof. No other sound. Enclosed by water and wind, Chinna and he could have been the only living beings on earth. If Zohra had been there he would have wanted nothing more, he would have wanted the rain to go on forever.

Nobody had seen the horse yet. For now it was his alone. The worry crossed his mind that it might crumble under the heavy rain, then he dismissed the thought—it was a sturdy, well-fired piece of work, and would survive gales, even hail. He began to wonder what he would do with it. Foolish not to have considered that he would need to store it somewhere, safe from his brother's avarice. From the start he had decided this horse would not be for sale and now, with the verses on it and their names, it was as powerful a symbol of their union as they would ever have, he and Zohra. He wanted to run out into the rain and down through the scrub to the pond just to look at it again, to marvel at his own work. He smiled in the dark. His head felt as if a hive of bees had been let loose in it. You are a potter, he told himself, learn patience. He knew he never would be patient, though making pots demanded it, clay needed time. It should have become routine for him by now, his urgency ought to have dwindled, but he was always in agonies of suspense in the last few hours to see how his pots had been changed by fire. And after the firing—why did it feel as if his terracotta horse might have trotted away from the side of the pond?

To calm down he placed a hand on Chinna to feel his deep, even breathing. He forced himself to close his eyes and by degrees the sound of falling rain cooled his fevered brain to sleep.

2

The blind calligrapher was the first to arrive at the pond the next day. He came with Zohra as soon as the rain had slowed to a drizzle, clothes soaking, cap plastered to his head, beard dripping water. He ran his fingers over the lines on the horse and exclaimed that the words in Urdu were so beautiful they had flowed onto the horse straight from Persia. Stealthily, because she never knew how well her grandfather could see, Zohra gave Elango's hand a squeeze.

Perhaps the calligrapher could not resist talking about the work he had done after his fallow years, or news just had a way of spreading. People from Moti Block began to appear later that day. The potter looked at them looking at his work and his eyes returned to his horse, not quite believing it was there—out from his dreams into the world. The once-mute daughter of the stonemason was gaping nearby and to his surprise he felt none of his familiar uncertainty around her. That morning she looked like any other child, small and wonder-struck, eyes shining with questions. He remembered how as a boy he used to climb onto the horses his grandfather made as soon as they were hardened in the firing, and all at once he picked up the girl and swung her onto the horse's back. She clutched its neck and rocked as though in her mind it had broken into a canter.

The rain came pouring down again and the people scattered. Over the next day or two, anytime the clouds gave way, a slow and growing crowd tramped through the mud and scrub to the pond. Word had spread that Elango had made a horse for the temple—the old kind that his grandfather had known how to make. The young had never seen one; the old began to reminisce about the holy processions, when decorated clay horses were wheeled around the neighborhood and everyone waited for a glimpse.

At the tea shop, Raju scented an opportunity and dispatched his brother with a soot-black saucepan and a stack of earthen cups. By the fourth day a man appeared with toys, balls, balloons, sweets for sale. Elango's friend Giri arrived, tortoise in hand, and grinned at him, saying, "You can charge a ticket price." He set down the tortoise. "I brought Hema Malini to see as well. Now wait, it'll take her all day and evening to reach the horse."

Elango observed the crowds, perplexed. Nobody normally ventured this far, to his pond, a place of contemplation and labor, and yet here they were, a procession of gawpers treating his sanctuary like a fairground. They would reach the edge of the forested land, where the pond shone in the clearing, and come to an abrupt halt. At about eight feet, the horse was taller than any of them. It had a headdress and a necklace made of raised beads of clay, its nostrils were flared. It was rounded and strong and though it did not look like a real horse there was something primitive and powerful about its flaring nostrils, its upright ears, the long pillars that were its legs.

On the fifth day, Vasu appeared with a stranger. You could hear his voice before you saw him. "It's for a hotel, you know. They are prepared to pay more than five thousand for it. It will be placed on a stand right in front of the hotel. Yes, of course he can make big elephants, even camels. My brother, he is a national artist. He went to show his work in Delhi. People come to his exhibitions. You think he makes only cups and pitchers? You're wrong."

Later that day, Sudhakar came, asking his way to the pond and stepping gingerly through the scrub.

"It's for nine thousand, that's what a big hotel is willing to pay," Vasu said. Sudhakar exchanged a look with Elango and edged toward him.

"Why should it be in a hotel?" someone said from the back. "This is a sacred horse. It can't be sent off to some hotel!"

A babble of voices rose with suggestions: Let's collect money for a festival right here. Everyone can donate. Let's decorate it with flowers and have a procession like old times.

Elango heard them out for a while, supremely good-humored. Nothing could ruffle him now that the work was done. He felt as if he had climbed a high mountain and reached the summit, lord of all he surveyed. He knew, and Zohra knew, what the horse meant, and that was all that mattered, he had come to think. If they wanted to take it to the temple, he would accept that. The horse would live alongside those made by his grandfather. In a sense, he thought, the temple was his horse's ancestral home.

He sat under the moringa tree that evening, smoking and running his fingers through Chinna's fur. Everything looked green and newly washed. The rain had been unusually heavy for their arid area and he luxuriated in the cool, damp breezes. The showers had made it messy too: black filth overflowing from drains in some places, pitted roads brimming with muddy water. But mud never bothered a potter.

He shut his eyes and sighed. He felt as if he had shed a great weight from his chest. What he had created came close to matching what he had imagined, which happened rarely. He wondered what his father would have thought, when he had worked so hard to raise his sons out from clay into the empyreal realm of ceiling fan, pen, ink. How old would his father have been today? He realized he had no precise idea of his father's age—he had been born to aged parents who had suffered the deaths of many children, and by his time there was no excitement left for the birth of another child, no records kept.

That night Vasu was in a good mood too. His customary truculence with Elango had softened for the moment into admiration. The horse brought back childhood memories of their grandfather's work, he said. He had never thought Elango had it in him to create anything as majestic. "Keep making these big things—horses, elephants," he said. "Forget teacups and pitchers. You were a fool all these years to waste time making those. Once people admit you are an artist, there's no end to the money we can make."

He grinned, he called Elango a secretive bastard, they drank rum. Giri overheard them and ambled across with Hema Malini. The minute he set the tortoise down, Chinna padded forward, intrigued and anxious. He slapped it with a paw. The tortoise became an immobile shell and Chinna frowned at it, ears flapping, nose twitching, bemused. Vasu yelled drunken encouragement. Inspired by the festivities, Revathi wrung the neck of one of her elderly roosters. Feathers flew, and she flung it into a pan with onions, garlic, chilies, drumsticks, tamarind, anything she could find, though generosity had its limits and she kept the talons aside to cook for herself later. She would burn away their few tiny feathers and stew them. She loved the crunch of them, claw by claw, then the gulping down of the gamy broth.

They ate her chicken and rice at almost midnight and nobody objected to the dog sitting nearby, attentive to every falling morsel. Across the wall next door, Akka sat alone. Her dark green sari was bunched up around her knees and her fingers were absently tying up limes and chilies to make charms, her ears trained on the loud talk and laughter next door. At least ten thousand, Vasu said. No, more than that, Giri said. If Elango managed to make a few more horses carved so beautifully with all that stuff nobody could read, anything was possible. Anything was possible with money, Revathi screeched from further away. They might buy out that old crone next door and make more space for hens, even a buffalo or two. Loud laughter. Vasu's voice saying they needed to drink to that. To be rid of that foul-mouthed witch. It was a dream that needed booze to feel real.

Akka felt black, scorching acid travel up from stomach to throat, into her mouth. She spat at the ground and wiped her mouth with a corner of her sari. They were mistaken if they thought they could scare her, a woman who had learned more about survival by living next to them than they could imagine. She would make a few visits the next day. First to old Taatha, then to the temple to tell the priests about a sacred horse desecrated with alien words.

3

Once, long ago, Elango would have said, if he were telling us this.

Once long ago a humble potter fell in love with a woman. They lived in the same neighborhood and he saw her every day, but he could not go up to her and tell her what was in his heart.

The man and the woman belonged to tribes that hated each other and he knew they could never be together. Then one night an earthen horse came to him in a dream, with flames at its nostrils and embers in its eyes and it spoke to him so clearly that he could hear each word. If he learned how to ride the burning horse on earth and under water, the woman would be his. He woke with the certainty that this horse had to be born and it was his job to give birth to it.

I saw Elango's horse on the sixth day after it was fired, when the sky cleared. Rain had settled the dust on the streets, washed clean every leaf, scrubbed the year-old grime off fences, gates, steps. In the cool, bright morning we went in a group from our cul-de-sac—Mrs. Khambatta, my mother, Tia, Gauri, my father too, and a few others, walking close together as if we were an army braving foreign lands. We had to walk down three alleys, pass Kummarapet, carry on down the road, then cross the long stretch of scrub to reach the pond. There was a trickle of people from the slums going in the same direction, saris and lungis hitched up to avoid the mud. Among us, only I had been to the pond before, but I could not confess as much, pretending surprise instead over every familiar sight.

As we approached I saw the smoke-blackened horse, its legs as massive as tree trunks. I had not expected it to be so big. I looked for Elango, feeling proprietorial. He was my teacher. I had come here when the horse was nothing but clay from the pond. I had helped to prepare the clay—not even Zohra could claim that. I was bursting to tell someone, but could not. My mother would be aghast I had been this far without permission. My father, liable to be more indulgent, was at a distance, talking to Elango.

There was a small crowd around the horse and as we stood there looking, two priests in white lungis appeared. A thin one with a fixed look of revulsion, and a bald, jowly one whose bare back was polka-dotted with black moles. Akka appeared hot on their heels, looking quite unlike herself without her usual basket for alms. She nodded briefly to my mother, went past me without a glance. Her disregard felt like the jab of a needle in the center of my forehead. My mind raced back to her questions a few days ago. She must know by now I had lied to her and it was certain that she would dream up some grim witchcraft against me.

She reached the priests standing before the horse, who were telling each other how this was the revival of a lost tradition and discussing the best way to move it to the temple. Akka began a slow walk around it as if circling a sacred idol, pausing at times for closer examination. She came to a standstill before the chest and the flanks of the horse.

"What is this writing?" she asked the thin priest after her long appraisal.

The priests murmured to each other. It was true, they had been looking at the design as lines, but indeed it appeared to be a script. Someone from the crowd said helpfully, "I hear it was carved by old Usman. Though he is blind. What a miracle."

"Urdu, then," the bald priest said.

"The language of poets!" someone cried out from the back.

"The language of mullahs," the thin priest said.

How could it be that a holy temple horse had been defaced this way? Akka asked the question once, then twice, then turned it into a chant. All at once she sank to the ground in the middle of the clearing, uncaring of the mud soaking her sari, and began beating her head with her hands and pulling at her hair until it became a disheveled mess. The red circle of kumkum in the center of her forehead spread across it like a wound as it was smudged by her fingers. She was sitting on the ground with her thighs wide apart beneath her sari and when she looked up her eyes were unseeing, except for one stray second when they rested on me, and then left my face. Her mouth opened into a huge black cavern which screamed, "Kill the potter. Break the horse. Each one who strikes a blow, God will know, God will know!"

For a few moments everything was very still except the tortoise inching forward—then Akka cried out those words again, louder. That was all it took for the people to be shaped into a mob, to shout, push, chant, shove, fall over each other.

I felt a hand grip my arm. My mother. I was being pulled away but we could not make much progress through the crowd, which pressed in on us. Akka was possessed by a divine spirit, someone nearby said. An angry spirit. She was on her feet now, whirling, lurching, and shaking as if she were having a fit. A space had cleared around her, even as the crowd swelled and surged toward the pond. My mother tried to barrel through in the opposite direction. She held my arm so tight I cried out for my father, but we could not see him anywhere, nor Tia.

"Break it down, it is evil," Akka chanted, swaying near the horse.

"Break it down, break it down," the crowd echoed.

"You fools," I heard Giri say somewhere near us. "Don't you want to know what is written on it? It's a poem by Kabir."

"I'll give you Kabir, sisterfucker," a voice roared. I saw a foot reaching out to kick Giri, send him flying. Another foot in his stomach, once, twice, and again.

I was dragged away by my mother. In that welter of people

I saw Elango in the mud, flailing, struggling to get up. A shoe came crashing down onto one of his hands.

His hands. Which he lived in fear of hurting. There was a shoe grinding into his hands. I broke free from my mother and ran toward him. Chinna had got there before me. A black-and-chestnut missile, the hackles on his neck rising like spikes. I saw his teeth sink into the calves of the man trying to break Elango's hands. A stick came crashing down on Chinna. Yelps of pain.

Then my arm was grabbed again and my mother was pulling me away. She had Tia with her as well now. We managed to reach an edge where we glimpsed bent, wizened Taatha, surrounded by men who half hid him from view. They held long iron rods of the kind used for building construction and moments later, he whispered something to them, and they began to advance on the horse. My mother clutched us hard, her arms over us like a shield. Other people stepped aside as the tall, burly men walked forward. They raised their rods and brought them crashing onto the horse. It was strong and hard, only a corner fell away, but it was the sign that impelled everyone to burst forward in a huge mass. Taatha stood watching and the ghost of a smile stretched his wrinkles when others in the crowd, who had contented themselves with chanting, scrabbled around for stones and other possible weapons. Someone sighted Elango's crowbar and his spade and swooped on them. More men appeared, the crowd swelled, they flung themselves into the business of battering the horse in an ecstasy of rage. The tail fell away. A leg broke in half and the horse tilted to one side.

"Each one who strikes a blow, God will know, God will know!" Akka cried out in her terrifying new voice.

A man further off discovered Elango's hiding place in the

lightning tree. The first thing he found was a piece of an earthen statue, then some potsherds. He flung them away. He rooted around deeper and from under a piece of cloth, the watch appeared.

"Look, look at this! That potter fucker is a thief too," he yelled.

". . . a watch! What else has he stolen?"

"Search that shed!"

"Search their house!"

"Kill the potter!"

"Break it down, they are evil!"

"Break it down, break it down."

"Each one who strikes a blow, God will know, God will know!"

Taatha's sharp quaver cut into the deranged shouting. "We can't have thieves living here. This is a neighborhood for decent people."

In the midst of it, we saw Giri stumble past holding his bloodied jaw with a wounded hand. I could not see Elango and began sobbing frantically, trying to tug my hand out from my mother's vicelike grip. Through moving slabs of people I saw someone pick up Giri's tortoise and fling it at the horse. It hit the hard terracotta and fell to the ground. You could not tell if it was a stone or a living thing. Someone shoved my mother to one side, she clutched me harder, shouting for my father in a voice I had not heard from her before or since, and there was a vast roar, voices indistinguishable, which echoed in my ears for days.

We got home after that, in ones and twos. My father had a bruised eye and his clothes were in tatters. Tia's dress was missing a sleeve. They did not know how it had happened. I have only a blurred recollection of running, falling, running again. An enormous hunger and thirst once we were home. I remember I fell into my bed, washed, changed, fed. I woke to an unearthly ocean-like glow. The setting sun shone onto my face through my blue curtains and when I pulled the curtains aside, the first thing I saw was that the guavas I had been monitoring for weeks on the tree outside my window were being pecked hollow by a pair of brown birds.

4

That evening our neighborhood was silent and dark but for the flicker of lights from television screens, though from a distance we could hear a low hum of raised voices and sounds of things breaking. If you didn't walk down the alleys but simply jumped over walls and trees there was only one line of houses between our quadrangle and Moti Block, where something seemed to be happening. My mother started locking the doors and windows as if that would keep a mob away. Elango lay in Tia's room. There were bandages on his head, on his right hand, and his left leg. Nothing was broken, he said with a weak smile when I went and stood by his bed. My father, an eye swollen shut, an arm bandaged, sat beside him. Zohra was pacing about, picking up books from Tia's shelf, opening them, slamming them shut, putting them back again. I had no recollection of a doctor coming, or how everyone had got to the house.

"We will never give them over to those hyenas," I heard my mother telling my father, who had said Taatha's henchmen were sure to arrive soon, looking for their prey.

A little while later I heard my mother's voice from the next room again. "How will we tell Elango?"

"You do it, I can't," my father said. "It has to be done."

With his uninjured hand, Elango was stroking Chinna's neck. He did not touch the blood-clotted fur on the dog's head, purple with iodine, which rested between his paws. If his hand slowed down or stopped the stroking Chinna raised his head to inquire. My mother appeared at the door and stood for a few minutes watching. The fan squeaked as it stirred up the humid air. From the next room we could hear music pouring in through the opened door. Long, rich notes. My father must have switched off his fan and was probably flat on his back on the stone floor with his eyes shut. He had the ability to disappear into his music, whatever happened—his angina pain, work troubles, any crisis at all.

Zohra looked up, saw my mother, and stopped pacing about. Elango tried to move.

"Chinna . . ." my mother began.

Chinna tilted his head to one side, as if following her every word. "If the dog barks when people come looking for you . . . it won't do. Everyone knows about him. We have to be very quiet."

Elango turned his face away.

"It is for your safety. I am just going to take him next door. He will be looked after," my mother said, and he nodded. At an awkward angle, he ruffled the fur at Chinna's neck and stroked him.

I went with my mother as she led the dog away through the back, across the lawn, and tapped on Mrs. Khambatta's window. Chinna's tawny eyes looked confused. The wound on his head was starting to seep blood again. He dug in his heels and pulled backwards. But together we were stronger than an injured dog and my mother murmured endearments and propelled him, by degrees, into Mrs. Khambatta's.

In Tia's room Zohra sat hunched beside the window, sobbing without a sound into the crook of her arms. Only her shaking shoulders told me she was crying. Tia went to her and stood close by, but Elango paid her no attention, rigid and fierce, as if he had locked himself away.

Late in the evening my mother ladled out the food Lakshmi had cooked and left. When Elango could not be persuaded to touch a morsel, my father sat next to his bed on a chair and started telling him about the book he was reading. I remember exactly what he said because he had told us these things so often.

The book was about igneous rocks that came from lava. Most of the Deccan plateau, where we were, was made of liquid rocks that had exploded from the belly of the earth and flowed over hundreds of thousands of miles, hardening over time. Such a very long time that you could not fit it into your mind. This land was a piece from the oldest continent on planet earth, did Elango know that? It used to be called Gondwana and before the shifting of the earth's plates it had been a part of Africa and Antarctica and Australia. More than sixty million years ago, volcanoes erupted here, one after another on an epic scale, laying down sediment, beds of lava, basalt, granite, flat as a tabletop. The eruptions might have killed off the dinosaurs, started a whole new phase of life on earth. From geological activity such as this had come potash and feldspar and quartz, and the clay with which Elango's pots were made. Someday—after this madness was over—they would go traveling outside the city, far into the countryside, to explore this giant plateau on which they lived, where they were not even a blink in the eye of planetary time.

Maybe he was not listening to a word, but these stories of rocks and fossils and plate tectonics had worked to soothe Tia and me and make us sleep, and now I saw Elango start to look like himself. He sat up against his pillow and ate a little, fumbling with his left hand. He lifted the steel tumbler and attempted to pour water into his mouth from a height, spilled it all over his shirt instead.

And then my father told him very gently that he and Zohra could not stay the night, for their own safety they would have to leave right away. Sudhakar was coming in a car to take them to his hotel. He would put them in a room there for a day or two, while he arranged for them to leave the city—temporarily, until the trouble subsided.

"But where will we go?" Elango said. "My home . . . my work . . . and the hotel won't allow Chinna . . ."

The rain carried on as if the sky were exploding. Over the sound of rain we could hear things shattering, a din of voices from the direction of Moti Block. The smell of burning was carried to us on the rainy breeze.

"It's better to take Chinna later," my father said. "Leave him with us just for the moment."

"How can we leave?" Zohra said. "My grandfather—I left him in Moti Block. What will happen to him? He can't see. He can't do without me." Her soundless sobs turned into huge gulps of breath, as if she were choking. My mother, who was not a hugging type, put an awkward arm around her shoulders and said, "The hotel is here in this town, not another city. We'll go to your house later and bring him here . . . and to the hotel tomorrow. But you aren't safe here any longer."

"This won't last," my father said. "A week or two. People forget."

I listened with steadily mounting panic to the talk flying back and forth. I looked at Zohra sobbing, at Elango rising from the bed, limping toward the door. You don't have to go, I heard myself say to him, what will I do without you down the road? We'll keep you safe in our house. I thought I said all those words and repeated them louder because Elango did not appear to hear anything, he was struggling to maneuver his injured left leg so his foot would fit into his slipper. Don't go, I thought I pleaded. Please don't go. I bent down and held the slipper so that he could push his foot in. He touched my head lightly once both his slippers were on and then he found his way out.

There was the sound of car doors. Low voices as Zohra and Sudhakar got into the car. For one long moment, Elango stopped. He hobbled back to our door as if he had forgotten something, paused, returned, and then turned again. What passed through his mind then, I could not know, maybe he thought he was abandoning his dog like those people on the highway. He had told us during our rickshaw journeys how he chanced upon the pup at dusk, thinking at first that its mewling was the sound of a forest spirit. How often had we heard the same story, as if his joyful disbelief at finding the love of his life in the middle of a forest could only intensify the more he spoke of it. It was mythical in our minds now, as well as his promise to the dog that they would never be parted.

I stood by the car in the rain. It poured down on me, it dripped into my eyes. The water trickled down to my lips, tasting briny. Tia was saying, "I think they'll never come back." My mother was saying, "Sara, come inside. You're soaking."

Sudhakar revved the car, told Elango to get a move on. Zohra stuck her head out of the window and said something. The last door slammed. Tires churned up the puddles. The wipers squeaked. And then quiet.

5

At Mrs. Khambatta's, Chinna raised his head and his ears flicked back and forth. The chestnut knobs of fur on his black forehead twitched like eyebrows. He sat up and whined. He padded across the house and scratched by turn at the two doors that led out and growled at them to open. He went back to the bed and stood beside it, whining louder and flapping his ears as he did to wake the potter.

Drowsy from her nightly sleeping pill and television, Mrs. Khambatta shook herself to life and patted Chinna absently, said, "Quiet, quiet," and when that did not stop the dog's cries, she began to stroke him and mumble a poem she had been made to memorize as a child. "Break-break-break, on thy cold gray stones oh sea," she said. "I would that my tongue could utter the thoughts . . . and the stately ships . . . what's next . . . and the stately ships go by and oh . . . um . . . and oh for the touch of a vanished hand and the sound of a voice that is still."

6

Today, I wonder at the certainty in these people that their world would heal in a matter of weeks. Were they hiding from the full horror of what had happened? It was not going to be a matter of weeks or even years. As the city was remade, Kummarapet itself would melt back to earth. New roads and buildings would replace its ponds, scrubland, hutments, tenements, the lightning-blasted tree, and the potter's clearing by it, until finally the very name of the village was erased from maps and it merged into the silent oblivion of the Deccan Plateau on which it had once lived.

Our own small community was to fall apart much sooner. When we promised to Zohra that we would look after her blind grandfather, we were not to know we would not find him at Moti Block, that he was not going to survive that night. Neither did we know that in two years Gauri, who used to sing romantic songs to her husband, would leave him and move to Canada with Mr. Wilson from upstairs, taking her two sons with her; in six years, Mrs. Khambatta would develop a wasting illness everyone attributed to Akka; in seven years Taatha would clear Moti Block for high-rise housing.

In five years, my father would be dead and we would be left with his photographic chemicals, his clothes, records, rocks and fossils, and an opened carton of cigarettes we found hidden away at the back of the junk cupboard, still giving out the scent of tobacco and old paper that to me was the particular smell of my father.

In five years and two months I would leave my mother and Tia and Chinna and step down from a plane onto another continent.

My father would have said change was the work of the earth spinning, spinning as it always had.

SEVEN

Wednesday, November 7

At my college I have a basic student room, but it has a rug on the floor, soft gray curtains on its two windows. On one side it overlooks the quadrangle with its grass and trees, and, on the other, the parking area. When I see the warm radiator in my room which makes it possible for me to be in a T-shirt, the air-light duvet that tousles my bed, the huge poster on the wall from Stratford-upon-Avon with a grim, bare-chested Coriolanus, I wonder how Fauzia is in her medical college hostel. She refuses to tell me why she returned home within a week of joining—my mother says she lay apathetic and uncharacteristically quiet, even had to be force-fed. Now she's back at her college again and writes bubbly letters embellished with ghoulish details about cadavers and organs and tells me with theatrical ennui about the endless rasam-rice meals and the bedbugs she shares her room with, as well as her real roommate. In her last letter Fauzia wasted a whole page on the roommate and what they did together as though they were the closest friends. I replied in kind, writing about Karin and the late-night movie we had gone to, the beer we drank afterwards at a pub. I know Fauzia has no access to pubs or to beer. I posted the letter before I could change my mind, cringed at my pettiness the moment the envelope was swallowed up by the mailbox.

(Later) I was sitting in my room, scribbling in my diary while waiting for the first sentence of a shatteringly brilliant essay to pop up by some miracle, when my door burst open and *enter Karin*, with flushed cheeks and damp hair. She dumped her backpack on the floor, pulled up my window, let in a rush of cold air, stuck her head out.

"Get up," she said, looking over her shoulder at me. "I feel like singing, come on."

I followed her, too accustomed to her oddities to be startled by anything. Outside the big glass window a milky mist had sucked the color from the trees and buildings. I could see shadows of people flitting down the walkways. It was too late for birds, too early for student stereos, and when Karin began to sing, her husky voice filled the courtyard. We stood there framed in the wide window, heads in the icy air, singing every song we both knew. When we got to her favorite, the one about the weather, beating the windowsill to keep time, someone from across the quadrangle joined in. Soon there was another voice and then another. And then the person in the room behind the beech tree began switching a red light on and off to the rhythm of the song.

"That's Miranda," Karin said. "She trains with me. Must've come back from her tutorial."

I've been at this place just over a month, though time is compressed here into an intensity that makes it feel much longer. Most people are still strangers. I don't know this Miranda-who-trains-with-Karin, but can see that mentioning her name fills Karin with energy. It made her slam the window down, and drag me out of my room. While I was laughing and protesting that I needed to pick up my jacket and keys, she was gone, hurtling down the walkway, out of sight in minutes.

I have no way of knowing what shaped her into this girl who appears and disappears at will. Days on end she doesn't come, and no explanation when she bursts in like this, maybe only because my room faces the courtyard and she needs to sing into it. Maybe the rigor of her athletic training makes her wilder when she is off duty. Early every morning as the days grow darker and shorter, if I stand at my other window I see her leave for the gym, cycling off down a road slick with rain. Hooded head sunk into her neck, waterproof jacket, legs in blue plastic rain pants. I know she'll go to the gym and start on a long workout. But this side of her life, maybe like many others, is unknowable to me. I have only recently found out that she can play the harmonica, and that she doesn't come to the pottery any longer because she has joined a choir. Last week, she lay on the floor in my room doing voice practice flat on her back, eyes closed, the same few notes over and over again. After Elango she is the only other potter I've known, but where it was the only way he knew to live, for her it is one of a hundred things she can do. Anything is possible for Karin here. She finds her own flightiness amusing. Flirts with new interests, tires of them once she divines their mysteries. The ground beneath her feet shifts its plates and she moves on, leaving no trace, not a single potsherd tucked away in a hollow tree.

Monday, November 12

Karin told me a couple of days ago that she had met someone at the choir. An astrophysicist who looked beautiful, she said, sang like an angel, and was doing research that would change the way the world looked at stars. Today she introduced us. His name is Darius; Parsis are all called Cyrus or Darius, he has told her, and when they aren't one of those two, they are Navroz or Feroze.

As Karin made the introductions, she explained in a teasing voice that the problem was Parsis were only allowed to mate with other Parsis so if anyone reported seeing them together to his relatives back home in Bombay he would be ostracized forever. The sun shone bright and ineffectual in a frozen blue sky, a boy and a girl walked past with hands snug in each other's hip pockets, but I saw that Darius maintained a studious distance from Karin even as he smiled indulgently at her. The thought crossed my mind that Elango and Zohra had to hide and wait and ultimately run away in order to be together. They had feared death, not social exclusion.

Darius has a grainy voice, tastes each word as he speaks, and there is an attractive diffidence about his slow, hesitant manner. He is at least a head taller than Karin though he has none of her muscle, and there's something awkward about him, as if his body has been assembled with more joints than necessary and he is liable to trip over his long limbs and fall any minute, like a puppet tangled in its own strings. His dark hair is longer than Karin's—to his shoulders—and the fingers of one hand keep tapping his other hand, playing a secret piano. His eyes never strayed far from her. He observed her with the entranced focus of a bird-watcher who has spotted a rare species. I wondered when—or if—anyone would ever look at me in that way.

His family had an apartment in a high-rise in Cuffe Parade,

facing the sea, he said, and every night he strolled down through Colaba to the Gateway to look at the lights on the water and have a cocktail at the Sea Lounge before heading home to listen to Yo-Yo Ma playing Bach. He has custom-built speakers made of wood that stand five feet high, and the valves for his amp come from Russia. It's the purest way to listen to music, apparently, this medieval technology of glass valves that glow red in the darkness. When he is done with his PhD here, he wants to go back and do nothing but listen to music with a glass of wine for company in his apartment, leaving it only to wander the roads, the *flâneur* of Kala Ghoda, for as many months as it takes to recharge his batteries.

I did not tell him about my only trip to his city, Bombay, nor of the evening when I had walked the Gateway trying to shut out the howling winds of terror inside me because suddenly my father was beyond my reach, anyone's reach. Darius's nostalgia and longing for that nightmarish city were unbearable, but I managed a pleasant, noncommittal answer.

I grow vile, I grow vile, I wear my real face behind a smile.

Cyclists clattered past us; knots of people crossed over to a craft fair in the garden of the church below which my pottery studio hid. I thought of my two round-bellied pitchers drying below our feet—the shelves must be exactly underneath where we were standing and they were waiting for me to come back and trim them. I started to fidget.

Ever since Karin met Darius I'm seeing much less of her. We have quick conversations in passing, like ants who pause on their busy routes to exchange notes with every other ant they meet. But she has stopped coming to the studio and hardly ever eats in college nowadays.

Saturday, November 17

I spoke too soon. Karin invited me to her room for dinner with the two of them, giving me a date and time. It sounded formal enough that I cycled off to a shop the day before and bought a bottle of red wine. I arrived gripping the bottle tightly by its neck, self-conscious at being invited this way to a room that I popped over to whenever I pleased. When Karin opened the door and stood aside to let me in, I saw she had dressed up: silk trousers, black shirt, a necklace of shiny beads. Her standard college room had been transformed into an exotic space with candles and perfume. Her Anglepoise lamp had gauzy cloth draped over it to disguise its sturdy efficiency. She had cleared away books and placed her study table in the center of the room. It was covered with something blue and gold. Darius was at the table, already high. He raised his glass to me and I nodded back, wondering irritably if he was going to be a fixture each time I met Karin.

She served us rice topped with fried egg and soy sauce, lemony chicken cut in slivers, soup. She held a bowl toward Darius and said ceremoniously: "This bowl is made with porcelain that I shaped especially for you, for this evening." She smoked, drank, and observed the two of us eating, but did not touch any of the food herself. At the end of the meal, she and Darius lounged on her bed, kissing and fondling each other, seemingly oblivious of me. Caution dissolved by wine and dope, he kept trying to put his hand up her shirt until, all of a sudden, Karin broke away from him as if she had remembered something and brought out a few white flowers from near the sink in her kitchenette. They were not flowers from a florist—they looked naked and defenseless, their bulbs hanging from them. Small bobbles of earth clung to the disinterred roots.

"Since you need no bowls, these are for you," she said. She flung herself onto the bed again, bunched Darius's hair in her hands, and kissed him.

The flowers looked like corpses next to the floor cushion I was sitting on. They looked as if they were decaying in the stuffy heat of the room with every passing minute. I could not fathom why she had given them to me, where she had found them, how she could make flowers look sinister. Their scent was nauseatingly sweet and my head swam with all the wine we had been drinking. When at last I was able to leave, I went back to my room through the garden instead of the sheltered corridors, needing to breathe cold, clean air, needing to throw the flowers away, as far into the black grass as I could.

Since yesterday, I've been going to the pottery every hour I have off from classes and libraries. I'm certain that Karin will not come here. In the studio I am back with my father and his rocks and minerals, and with Elango. His voice is in my ears as I pick up a pot from my shelf that I made the day before and I tap it gently, trimming tool in hand.

See how the clay is firm enough to hold its shape but soft enough to let you work on it. This is when you can transform it. Make it your own.

I place the pot on the wheel, it starts spinning and clay comes away from it like cheese parings as I run my tool over its sides. The pot is leather-hard—neither damp nor dry.

You are like that pot right now. Old enough to understand but young enough to learn—how old are you? Thirteen? One day you'll be so grown-up you'll think you know it all. Your hands will have set ways to move. Let's see how long you can stay young enough to learn.

I am trying to work out how old Elango was when he taught me. How young has he stayed in the five years since I last saw him? Is he still learning or only teaching?

And I wonder if I will ever see him again.

Tuesday, November 20

My mother's latest to me keeps as always to the quotidian— garden news, neighborhood gossip, stories from the editorial desk at her newspaper—things she considers safe, not liable to upset my equilibrium while I struggle (as she thinks of it) with alien scholarship in a language I thought I knew. She is trained as a reporter and news writer, and her habitual steel cage of facts and word limits keeps her from wandering into dangerous bogs of feelings, regrets, confidences. Whatever her own battles with loneliness or grief or Tia, her struggles with the will my father never got around to making and his withheld pension, she tells me nothing. I can imagine that well-meaning people suggest she join embroidery clubs, find an accountant, take singing lessons. I am sure my mother ignores such advice, turning more and more stubbornly solitary in order to sidestep their compassion, listening to my father's old records, eating TV dinners with Tia, going to work.

She writes that a few days after I left, Chinna crept into her bed for the first time. When my mother stroked him, he shifted to another part of the bed to escape her touch but did not go too far. Later that night he came back and nuzzled my mother under her chin, then curled up against her and slept the night through. This was reported to me as a triumph.

Chinna's personality altered after Elango left our neighborhood. Not immediately. At first he would wander off and go one by one to his usual stops: Sharma-ji's shop, the pond, Elango's house. But his nose said each place was different, the scents had changed. From food, drumstick trees, earth, and water to the stink of burning and destruction. The pond was a mess of broken and charred things and Taatha had thrown out Vasu and Revathi and muscled into their burned-down house, flattened the ruins. They had fled the neighborhood for the other side of town, managing to take with them only a few hens, their clothes, and the table fan.

For several days after Elango vanished, Chinna wandered like a demented dog, not coming home even to eat, then turning up bloodied from dog fights, muddy and defeated, to collapse in a corner of our courtyard. We washed him with warm water, dabbed him with iodine, fed him soft food. The routine was repeated the next day and the next. He was tireless in his search and we did not know how far he went on his trail. He was not to know that his friend had decided not to return. Elango telephoned from the hotel to say Sudhakar was sending him to Delhi and funding him to do a formal course in ceramics so that he'd be able to find a job at a studio.

"You'll come and see us before you go . . . at least for Chinna . . . ?" my mother said, when he phoned.

"I can't take him with me . . . why get his hopes up? I won't come." He had hung up abruptly.

I had thought it unbelievably cruel of him to leave without saying goodbye, even wondered if he had ever loved the dog. Since then, having waited in the hospital mortuary for my father to open his eyes so I could tell him everything I urgently needed to, I've come to know well the agony of parting without a chance to say goodbye.

In the end, Chinna stopped searching for Elango, and even stopped going toward Moti Block. He was no more the dog-about-town whom everyone laid a claim to, who smelled so strongly of the world outdoors he needed to be doused with soap and water every day. Overnight, his muzzle seemed to be sprinkled with white, his steps became a little slower. More and more, we found him on our front veranda all day, keeping a watchful eye out for Elango in case he returned, but not leaving again to look.

Only at night would he leave the veranda and come in. Where he had always kept his distance, he began to slip into my father's bed. The two of them slept close to each other, breathing each other's breath—as I suppose he had done with Elango.

Now that my father was gone, he was having to get used to my mother.

Maybe, as the child of my mother, I tell her nothing much either. My letters home are like excited dispatches from a new world, a diary of infinite possibilities, descriptions of places and people. Amusing reports on my fumbling pottery and the idiosyncrasies of my supervisors. The monotony of dining hall food. Nothing about the way I followed a man through the streets the other day because the set of his shoulders and back were so like my father's that I could not stop walking behind him until he turned to stare me down and broke the spell. Nor do I tell Amma I am struggling with my studies, of my shock at finding that, though I was at the top of the class at home, here I am average. When I read Shakespeare or Sylvia Plath at home, the texts were unreachable or exotic in the same way to everyone. Here I am the odd girl out—the others doing the English literature course are either British or American and they seem to share from birth a set of codes that will always be barred to me. I've made a terrible mistake coming here, I'm wasting the Abdulali Trust's money, I should be doing something else. Making pots, dreaming up a horse. Anything to save me from Milton's unearthly vision of fucking paradise lost. In some ways, everything's easy here, it's a do-what-you-want place, people are mostly kind, but there's something else—they invite you over but seem to disinvite you in the same breath, they smile at you at lectures one day and look through you the next, their voices and bodies are modulated to make you feel excluded. It isn't paradise lost, it's a paradise that is also purgatory.

All of this is a set of jumbled, indefinable sensations, unsayable to anyone, especially in an aerogram home. Most of all, I don't tell my mother about the film that plays inside me on a loop. It shows, scene by scene, an argument with my father in the days before he went to the hospital. He had wanted my help to catalog his fossils and I wasn't in the mood for a talk on geology. I told him it could wait.

"It can't wait, because I have to go to Bombay," he said. "Bring down the boxes. It won't take long, I need to put them in order before leaving. Call Tia too."

"I have homework, I have to meet my friends in one hour for a movie, I can't sit around right now looking through *rocks*! Don't you understand? Rocks won't run away! We'll do it another time, after you're back."

"Maybe I won't be back," he had said, so quietly I should not have heard it.

His words and his voice came back to me in the middle of a concert last evening, and I felt tears on my cheeks though nothing had happened to make me cry. I had forgotten to bring tissues and had to keep wiping my nose and eyes on my sleeves or the back of my hands. The woman next to me leaned as far away from me as she could. The chapel glowed and shimmered with flames from candles and chandeliers and around me were evening gowns and suits, people who appeared to know each other. I had come alone, on an invitation from Karin. A special front-row ticket to Handel's *Messiah* at one of the college chapels and she would not hear of a refusal. She had told me she would see me there. When I reached the main doorway, she was nowhere, so I went in and took my seat, expecting her to slide into the empty place next to mine. She did not appear.

I was about to leave when it was announced that a junior choir would sing before the main performance. They listed the songs, described the novelty of Schubert's "Ave Maria" being sung by a choir when it had been written for a solo voice, they went on about its versions, but I heard very little, looking at the singers file in, seeing Karin among them, unrecognizable in a dark blue silk dress. She had said she would see me there, and she was as good as her word: she looked straight at me as she sang. Darius stood in the row behind her. Their voices rang through the church, weaving ceilings, walls, stained-glass windows into one. They sang as if they had always drawn every breath together. For how many days had they practiced, laughed, talked, sung together to reach this point? After the sessions they must have spilled out onto the frozen streets in a clamor of shouted plans and whispered secrets, wound their way to a pub, and sung noisy, non-Schubert songs before heading back to college, treading softly past the lit windows of the library where they might have glimpsed me bent over books, trying to make sense of printed words . . . Individually words had dictionary meanings that I was familiar with and yet when they were ranged together in a sentence and the sentences in paragraphs in my new books on critical theory, they broke rank, refusing to add up to meaning.

Thursday, November 22

Yesterday I woke up to my deadlines and realized in the studio that I had to hand in my weekly essay on tragedy in a day's time, but hadn't written a sentence so far. I went into a trance of panic, but was still unable to leave and go to the library. I sat hunched over the wheel, making bowls, cylinders, bottles, whatever my fingers wanted to do, in my head trying to disentangle *Glass Menagerie* from *Elektra* and *Antigone* until it felt as if my hands were moving without thought or plan, the clay was rising, falling, and forming of its own volition. I could hear the *plop-plop* of water from a tap I hadn't turned off. An announcer on the radio predicted icy conditions and dangerous roads, urged everyone to stay indoors. The news began and went on about Margaret Thatcher and the bomb last month at her hotel in Brighton. With a brave tremor in her voice, she had said, "Life Must Go On," and the radio played that back every now and then, as if trying to convince us what a narrow escape it had been.

And then there was someone else in the studio.

A curious sense came over me that the room was vibrating, as if every tool and machine and pot had the electric charge of life, that they were breathing, waiting. I could see nobody there, but I was aware of somebody. I didn't dare turn to look, I didn't move a muscle, yet I began to feel unaccountably alert, each of my nerve endings separately alive. I became conscious of a rhythmic squeak from the wheel I was working, I could see my hands rising in tandem within and outside the pot I was making until they met at its lip, and all along I did not dare look over my shoulder or anywhere else for fear of losing the invisible person with me in the room. The low voice on the radio had changed to mysterious, murmured nonsense: " . . . the general synopsis at 1800 high two hundred miles west of Bailey 1027 expected fifty miles to the north of Shetland. High Plymouth 1021 dissipating. Low Fitzroy 1011 losing its identity . . ."

The shipping forecast ended, the vibration surrounding me wound down, and the basement began to feel like itself again. I stopped the wheel and rested my hands on the cool, solid clay. I turned the wheel on again and three perfect bowls took shape between my fingers without a second's struggle. I had made myself a gauge of the kind Elango had taught me, crossing two thin sticks, and I realized I had effortlessly made each of the bowls the same diameter and depth. I had fallen out of practice in the past five years and my newfound ease made me so lighthearted I danced to the music on the radio as I cleaned and washed up, placing my new bowls on my shelf in an orderly row.

When I came up from there into the early evening above ground, there was something rushing downward from the sky that looked like rain but wasn't. A fine spray of white covered the saddle of my bicycle. It was icy on my face. There was a man unchaining his bike next to me and I asked him, "Is this snow?"

"Sleet," he said. He put up his jacket's hood and cycled away.

I stood still in what I now knew to be sleet, feeling it cover me and my bike and my clothes. The streets were empty and almost dark, people were walking fast, faces down. The headlights of cars shone on the road. A sharp wind cut through my jacket. Nothing had changed and yet, inexplicably, the cold was bracing instead of numbing, the darkness promised long hours of warmth and reading, and the way ahead was uphill, but my legs and lungs did not complain.

I cycled up the hill thinking not about my unwritten essay but of an evening some weeks after Elango was driven out of his home. We had gone to the pond later and salvaged as much of the broken horse as we could, and every day after work, my father sat with terracotta pieces spread out on the dining table, putting them together. I usually helped and we worked on the fragments as if on a jigsaw puzzle. That day my father, carefully squeezing out beads of glue from a tube of Quick Fix, said, "Tia told me you've been waking up at night crying in your sleep."

"No, I'm not," I said. "She talks such rubbish."

"She does?"

"She has to make a drama out of everything. I must have had one bad dream."

"And what about making pots? That's all stopped. Maybe I can make you another wheel to practice at home—or you'll forget everything you learned."

"I don't want to make pots again. Ever." I felt tears pricking the corners of my eyes, and my nose started to water.

He gave me a considering look, then asked me to pass him another fragment of the broken horse. "Where do you think that goes? Could it be a part of this ear . . . ?"

As we joined the pieces to form the head of the horse, he started talking to me. At first of this and that. His climbs in the mountains, the prospecting for minerals. An elephant that with his massive trunk gave their tent a gentle swipe, toppling it. Then he talked about the riots people had to flee during Partition, the killings after mere cricket matches. I felt myself contracting at the thought that he was about to remind me how I had forgotten Tia in junior school and run back home. But I realized he was trying to explain what had happened to Elango and his horse. He said that was the thing about religion: it could lead to a kind of insanity. Fanatics needed no provocation and Akka would have found out about the thing Elango was making at the pond even without the information I had given her, and if not the horse, she would have found some other means to destroy him. If she had not declared war on him and Zohra, someone else would have done it. Muslims and Hindus—it wasn't so much about religion as a blood feud like *Romeo and Juliet*.

My father dipped matchsticks into a puddle of glue, puzzling out how the pieces fitted, and by the end of that evening we managed to restore almost the entire head of the horse. We put it on display before my mother came back from the newspaper office and she entered the room and gasped with astonishment. The head was still missing an eye and a cheek and it took up most of a windowsill in the living room like a dented but determined sentinel. My mother placed a trailing plant next to it to hide the broken ear. I started to feel lighter, happier, more like myself. I forgot to blame myself for a few hours. I didn't move the food around my plate, I ate it instead. That night for the first time I slept deeply and sweetly till the morning without nightmares of Akka and the pond, of running after her to stop her from going there, falling over Elango to save his hand from being pulverized. I woke up absolved.

I had the same feeling as I walked away from the studio yesterday. A new lightness and clarity. As if a fog had lifted from my brain and I could see the narrator in "The Glass Menagerie" egging me on, waiting for me to finish writing my thoughts on him and turn the essay in. "The play is memory," he says, as if speaking directly to me. "Being a memory play, it is dimly lighted, it is sentimental, it is not realistic. In memory everything seems to happen to music. That explains the fiddle in the wings. I am the narrator of the play, and also a character in it."

Tuesday, November 27
Dr. Golde had a meltdown during our supervision. We are five—she fixed her gaze on each of us by turn and said she was uniformly unimpressed by the profundities we had spewed out on the topic "Wild laughter in the throat of death: Discuss." Our essays were in an untidy pile on her coffee table. She jabbed them with her pen and said, "I can see five Thirds here."

She's a woman of (at least to us) immense age—older than anyone I have ever known. She went off to be a nurse during the Spanish Civil War, and her lover fought on the Republican side and was killed by a bomb. This is part of history for me, not real life. I wonder if she knew Neruda or Lorca but she doesn't talk about any of this despite the embers in her eyes, glowing with unsaid things. She's said to have been a great beauty and despite her asthmatic breathing she still has a stern elegance about her—skin like crazed bone china, and improbable chestnut hair that flows to her waist. Today, something Annika said about being bored with the "silly old doll-playing" in "Glass Menagerie" flicked a switch in Dr. Golde and she thumped our stack of essays and wheezed, "All of this . . . every page here . . .

is a waste of ink and paper. What can you know until you have lived? What can you know about death or life or laughter? You. Cannot. Know. Anything. At your age!" After each word she had to stop to draw breath and the sound of it would come from deep inside her like a soft, high-pitched scream. After she finished, her coughing went on and on.

I began to worry she would collapse right there, but (over her coughing) Annika retorted that Tennessee Williams was only thirty-three when "The Glass Menagerie" premiered, so he was old, but not *ancient*. Dr. Golde recovered enough to wheeze something cutting in reply and a heated discussion carried on until our hour was over.

As I cycled back to my college I tried to imagine myself getting into an argument with Begum Tasneem. I thought of the lilies in her room, the cool appraisal in her look, and the deference in ours, and knew that, however belligerent Annika sounded and however intimidating her lip stud and leather jackets, Begum Tasneem would not have allowed her to say another word. She would have been waved to the door in under a minute for insolence. For the first time in two months, I found myself singing as I cycled, felt the pure blue of the morning sky fill me. The days ahead were infinite, they were filled with boundless possibilities, I did not have to be virtuous or grateful or frugal, I could get myself neon tights like Karin's and I could tell Dr. Golde all that I knew of laughter in the throat of death.

Wednesday, December 12
The Christmas break has started, college is mostly empty, and the wind seems to be blowing straight from the gulags. A few

hours ago, Karin brought in the cold—she came into my room in jacket, beret, boots and began to unpeel layers of damp outdoor clothes even as she turned on my kettle for tea. She paced around with the tea, spilling it on her clothes each time she laughed too hard. She was chattering about St. Ives, which she had just come back from, the shop where she bought a key ring that said Karen because they stocked no Karins, the sea crashing against the coast nonstop, how she ate sweet popcorn for the first time in her life.

After several minutes of babble, she stopped and announced she had broken up with Darius—just over a month into her relationship, she was rid of him. She said she still had not slept with him—her weekend away was when it was supposed to happen, but on the train there, watching him sit a discreet distance from her in case the train contained Parsis who might send home reports about him, then smooth a napkin over his knees so that his clothes would not be littered with sandwich crumbs, she started to feel all her attraction for him turn inexplicably to its opposite. The more he praised the dark skies over Bodmin Moor and deplored modern electric lighting that outshone stars, the more absurd she found him. She mimicked his tone, his undecided way of speaking.

Could I imagine the horror of it, she said, giggling convulsively, a dirty weekend with Darius the virtuous? Those two days by the sea he forgot all about other Parsis and kept clinging to her, trying to be amorous, hoping she would pull down her knickers for him. He was that last bit of scotch tape you simply cannot shake off, she said. He clung to her waist and nuzzled her ears until she felt she would go mad. Everything he did, including things that used to endear him to her, began to annoy her, then infuriate her, until she could stand it no longer, she would choke if she had to breathe the same air.

I listened to her, thinking this confirmed my ideas about the nature of the cosmos, that it's hell-bent on doing things we can neither anticipate nor prevent. When the stars are in a good mood they send signs—white sleet comes down from black skies, gray and pink minerals turn into depthless blue-green glazes, submarine horses in dreams gallop the floors of silent seas breathing fire. But mostly the stars send stop signs or breakdown signs.

Karin tossed a packet of photographs onto my bed and said, "I should have gone with you. There were so many pottery shops. There was the Leach Pottery too. And there was this show there, out in the open. I wanted to look at it, but bloody Darius wouldn't give me a minute."

They had booked a double room, she said, and she could not afford to get a separate one for herself alone. Condemned to sharing a bed, she turned the other way to sleep, but still he pulled up her T-shirt and pushed his damp penis into her back. She found herself yelling at him in Chinese, which she had not spoken since she had left Malaysia. She pushed him away with both hands. She had not kept in mind the strength that years of weight training had given her, nor had she remembered how thin he was. He fell off the bed groaning and cursing, clutching his belly, yelling that she had killed him. They had come back on different trains.

While Karin rattled on, I looked at the photographs. They weren't holiday photos and there were none of the two of them together or apart. There was a gray, aggressive sea, jagged rocks, compositions of light and shade, a little art deco village cinema hung with fairy lights for Christmas. And a set of huge animals, ranged together like a terracotta army. An elephant, an alligator. A dog. The dog was looking up at a horse. There was something elegant and powerful about their stylized shapes, the designs on their bodies. One of the elephant close-ups contained the figure of a man, lean and brown, who was in the photograph by sheer chance. The hair was clipped too short for me to be able to tell if there were still curls but that face and the oddly intense gaze . . . I would have known those anywhere. It was Elango.

She peered over my shoulder. "Oh yes," she said, "I thought you'd like those. They had beautiful script on them. Darius said Arabic."

I got up and went to the set of shelves in my room. Among the books was a piece of pottery. It was one of our salvaged pieces from Elango's broken horse. Apart from the head my father and I had pieced together, other fragments we had retrieved were in the backyard at home. Two of the legs were planted by the guava tree and the tail served as an arch above the birdbath. Tia used one of the hooves as a doorstop.

I took the piece from my shelf and another shard I always kept in my pocket or the bag I was carrying, as a talisman. It held two strokes of the calligrapher's carvings.

"Did the design work on those animals look like this? Was that an Indian? Where is he now? Do you have his name?"

"How would I know if he's Indian? I've got a leaflet somewhere . . . unless I've lost it." She shrugged as if already bored.

I told her to sit still for a few minutes, that I had to tell her why it was important. I told her about Elango, about Zohra, about the horse and how it almost got them killed. I talked about my father dying in a hospital, out of our reach, alone in an intensive care ward. I told her I had thought I was to blame for what happened to Elango and how my father had convinced me it was not my fault.

When I finished, she got up from the bed and went to make more tea. I could hear cup and spoon clattering and then her voice, uncharacteristically wistful. "If I had your dad instead of mine, I'd be happy I had some good years with him. So what if they were very few."

She turned to me with a merry grin and two mugs of tea. "I know you'll be shocked," she said. "But I've lost count of the times I've wished my dad would kick the bucket. Bloody man is immortal. He'll stick around till I give him a gold medal to pack into his coffin. But now—how do we find this horse maker of yours? Was he actually the guy in St. Ives? How do we confirm that?"

I took a framed photo down from the top of my cupboard. Tia and me in the auto-rickshaw. Elango looking back over his shoulder at Chinna squashed between us. My father had taken the picture from somewhere near the front mirror of the auto-rickshaw to fit all of us into the frame.

"That's him, I think it is," Karin said. "Wait, I'll look for the leaflet. You need to find him."

Thursday, December 13
That was yesterday, and with my mother five and a half hours ahead of my clock it was too late to phone her. I had to wait until after midnight to call. She was just about awake—I could picture her, porcupine-haired, rushing to the phone, panicking that it was ringing so early. She calmed down when she heard my questions. She had already written to me about Elango going

to Britain, she said in a tone of righteous indignation. Yes, she admitted she had (yet again) forgotten to post it, but really, her letter was on its way, with news of how Sudhakar had phoned the other day after an eternity, saying her paper ought to do a feature on Elango, he was going places. Someone from the French embassy had seen his terracotta animals at an exhibition in Delhi, which resulted in a trip to France for a festival. After that he had done a workshop in Sweden, teaching potters how to make his kind of sculptures, and now he was in Britain. "Sudhakar was so proud," my mother laughed, "just like I am when I talk about you. If you find him, take a picture of him. And give him a scolding. Why hasn't he ever been in touch?"

The information in Karin's leaflet places him in London from Friday—his pieces will be on display at a gallery and he is going to teach students at a workshop for a few weeks. The scholarship money for my first term is running out fast, plus I am saving to travel in the summer. But I know I must go and see him. The good thing is I've managed to win a travel grant from my college and I can use that money right away.

I cycled down from my college to the bank later in the morning and checked how much money I had in my account, went on to the train station to buy a ticket. As I was coming back from the station I passed a row of shopwindows, one of them with a mannequin in a dark blue anorak with a hood. The jacket had a soft exterior, many pockets, dull metal buttons, and a fleece-lined hood. I stopped pedaling and jumped off my bike. I clutched my wallet fat with money fresh from the bank. It felt like a warm piece of reassurance in my pocket. I knew I needed to make it last. I thought I shouldn't . . . but there was no harm looking. I chained my bike to a stand and went across to the shop, saw the price, instantly walked away almost to the end of the road. I could not afford it. In seconds I went back and before I could think too hard I had gone in and paid for the jacket.

Monday, December 17

It's too big. The blue works, though: when Elango put it on, it set off the polished-wood color of his skin and intensified the new flecks of gray in his hair.

"I didn't know what size to get," I said.

In the charcoal coat he was wearing when I came upon him smoking outside the gallery he would not have been out of place in one of those dark films where the hero is destined for trouble. But the anorak diminishes him somehow, with its baubles and brass. Its sleeves are too long. The shoulders droop. I had always thought of him as tall and broad, my memory of him was of a man who swung me into his auto-rickshaw when I was little as if I were a small bundle he was lifting. When I stand next to him now, my head reaches his shoulders and he is thin, his body is like wire twisted into angles for shape.

There was something fumbling and embarrassed about our meeting at first. Having no way of contacting him, I had not told him I would be coming and I could not tell if he was annoyed or pleased to see me. He had no trouble recognizing me and stubbed out his cigarette as if I were still a little girl he could not smoke with. He peeled himself away from the wall he was leaning against and said something I was too muddled to register. Before we had exchanged two sentences, I had given him the jacket, to fill up the space where no words were possible.

His face gave nothing away when he took it. He fiddled with it, pulling a string here and a pocket flap there. I began to think it was the wrong thing to have bought. I felt watched and jumpy with his terracotta menagerie around us, an assortment of animals staring with their sightless eyes. Their legs are long, their bodies are rough and primitive, the script that travels over the surfaces looks like an ancient code. People walking rapidly past us slowed down, then edged closer to the animals as if drawn into an invisible force field. One man said the writing on them was in Hebrew, his friend disagreed and claimed in an authoritative voice it was Tibetan. The first man said the animals had a tinge of ancient Mayan about them, but were imitative. No, no, more like the Trojan horse, said his friend.

I must have been glowering at them because Elango said, "Sara flies into rages, she stamps her feet, that's what your sister used to say. That hasn't changed in five years?"

He pushed the anorak's hood onto his head. His face retreated, as if into a cave. "Only a woman would cover her head this way at home." He began to laugh, his eyes and cheeks creased in the old way and he said, "I would never have bought anything so expensive for myself, and you shouldn't have either."

The people milling around us had moved further away, toward the dog and the panther. The alligator's row of teeth and ridged back must have taken days to put in place, I could hear someone say. Another voice said the dog did not look like a dog and the cat looked more like a leopard. I pulled the hood of my own jacket over my head, and turned away from the sculptures toward him to find that he had turned toward me at the same moment. We looked at each other from within our warm shells. Something seemed to shift, sigh, settle into place.

He said, "It's big enough to be a blanket. I will wear it, sleep in it, live in it."

From my backpack I drew a small bowl I had made.

"I'm practicing . . . I didn't make anything at home after you left. Thought I'd forgotten everything but now I'm starting to remember."

I watched him run his fingers down the inside to see how evenly I had thrown it. "Who would have thought?" he said, raising an eyebrow. "Our little Sara has become a real potter. No, you can never forget, you started learning so early. It's like breathing for you . . . your body knows what to do."

Elango is making two eight-foot-tall horses at the gallery, with about fifteen students. There are also two archaeologists observing the process, because they have only ever seen ancient terracotta potsherds and they want to understand the process of making those pots. He has an interpreter who translates back and forth for him from Telugu and Hindi into English. He took me to where the workshop was, and before starting he stripped down to a T-shirt and shorts, the way I remembered him. For four hours he was a whirling dervish, swooping from one student to another, directing the preparation of the clay inside and supervising the construction of a special gas-fired kiln outside. One of the horses is being made with stoneware clay instead of Elango's usual low-fired terracotta and will become the centerpiece of the gallery's garden. It will have to be fired to almost thirteen hundred degrees Celsius. To reach that temperature, the room-size kiln would need to burn for two entire days, Elango thought, and who knew if the horse would survive such prolonged incarceration? In asides he forbade the interpreter from translating into English, he said to me, "If this goes wrong, I'm finished. What if it explodes? What if the kiln doesn't reach that temperature? I'll need more than a horse to run away on."

Friday, December 21
A lot to remember and put down before I forget. I am only just back in my own room. Ended up spending five days in London. The nights were in a sleeping bag in a friend's hostel room in Russell Square, and early each morning I would go to the gallery, notebooks in a satchel. When Elango wanted to talk, I took notes. When he had to work, I rolled up my sleeves, put on an apron, and plunged my hands into the clay. If he wanted a break we went for walks down the crowded streets toward a nearby park, which was no more than a square with leafless trees under a sky that looked like frozen lemonade.

On the two or three sunny days we got, we ate our sandwiches in the park, needing the air and emptiness after his packed hours of teaching. He wanted to drink bottle after bottle of beer, he thinks it makes him warmer. I saw him use fork and knife in the American way: he cut up all the food methodically, then stabbed each piece with his fork and put it into his mouth, grumbling, "Why can't these people use their fingers? Do they stroke each other with a fork and knife too?" We ate pizzas so he could use his fingers. I bought him chili flakes to sprinkle on them. After a long day of teaching, he would be ravenous and I felt myself smiling, looking at him gobble like a child. I realized that I had thought him a lot older than me, but he must have been only in his midtwenties when I used to learn from him. The minute that thought crossed my mind, I got up from my chair, went to the women's room, washed my face in cold water, tied my hair back again, and scowled at myself in the mirror before going back to him.

We played at being tourists too. One afternoon we went in a boat down the Thames to Greenwich. Christmas lights sparkled in the trees along the riverbank. He wore his new jacket, sleeves folded back from his wrists, hood over his head, and stood in the prow of the boat until he was ordered to take a seat. We searched out ceramic collections in museums and I decoded the captions for him when he had problems with the English. We walked by the river and he touched every twisted lamp post on the Embankment as if he were telling them he had come. When he was not teaching but out wandering, there was something of the waif about him, a boy who might have come from nowhere and had never stopped believing in signs and wonders. Back in my room now, with my bleak poster of Coriolanus and stacks of unread books from the library, I keep daydreaming about the sheer, uncomplicated happiness of the last week and wish I had stayed longer.

When I took lessons from Elango all those years ago, I took his skill for granted. He made it look easy, as if spinning out pots was a natural function of the human body. Watching him now, the brown of the clay and of his hands appeared to be one—as if he were pouring himself onto the wheel and turning into any shape he willed. His palms, his thumbs, his fingertips seemed to caress, support, hold, and draw up the clay, knowing exactly what it was seeking at different times. At work in this way he was utterly absorbed, barely aware of me even when I was sitting just a few feet away. He can be—he is—alone wherever he is, and I wonder how Zohra deals with this. He showed me a picture of her: she looked much as I remember. Thin face, huge eyes, scar interrupting an eyebrow, collarbones that jut out, and a small pendant at her neck. It was a photograph of the two of them, taken after their wedding in a courthouse with Sudhakar trebling as witness, photographer, only guest.

At the London gallery he has constantly to work with people—suppliers, mechanics, students, the owners of the gallery. As soon as I entered the room, the hum of the wheels, the quality of the subdued chatter would tell me what sort of temper Elango was in. His moods dictated the atmosphere and they seem to change more than I remember. In the days I spent there, I saw that when he was cheerful and humming songs, the most dour of the students started to smile; but a cloud settled over the place during the times he snarled and found fault, telling them to go find other work in a language they could not understand, but whose sense his tone made crystal clear. The black ink floods into him. He mutters. I know from the time I used to learn with him that his caustic remarks and demanding manner are just the other side of his certainty about his students' gifts. They don't know that.

Away from other people, he told me how hard the first few years had been. The days in the Deccan Gold Hotel, Zohra and he, isolated in an uncomfortably shiny room, plagued by the image in his head of his dream destroyed, living on Sudhakar's charity. What an ideal honeymoon, could any couple have asked for more! He didn't laugh, the recollection was still bitter. The journey to Delhi with Zohra in tears over her grandfather. The yearlong ceramics course. Sudhakar paying for everything.

"Why didn't you come and see us after you left?" I said. "People with rods and sticks barged in looking for you. We thought they would kill us. My father never got to see you again, and he was so fond of you."

"I was afraid," he said after a long silence. "And then, for so many years, moving from one place to another. Many people would not rent us a room once they knew she was Muslim, and the others wouldn't when they knew I was Hindu, and some thought we'd eat pork at home, and some thought we'd cook beef . . . I never understood how bad it could get until Zohra came into my life. We kept moving. Trying to find work. I had no money for train tickets, we hardly had enough for rent and food."

"But didn't you want to see Chinna? You could have written to us."

As soon as I mentioned Chinna, it was as if someone had rolled the shutters down on Elango's face. He bought time by lighting a cigarette. We were walking in St. James's Park and he turned back to me to point to black swans gliding about in the lake below the bridge. He said it was time to leave if we were not to be late for the afternoon class.

"When things go wrong, they go really wrong . . ." he said, walking back. "Suddenly Sudhakar abandoned us too. No answers to letters, and his hotel only said he had left . . . I had no idea what he was up to. The money from him stopped coming. The course he'd paid for was over. I had learned all about real kilns, glazes, raku, stoneware, porcelain. Learned my way around studios. But didn't have money for even a shed or space for pit firing."

"What did you do?"

Elango grinned. "If there's one thing I can do it's work. Big studios hire laborers. You'll see when you join one. There'll be underfed, murderous wretches with burning eyes working the clay, cleaning, unloading supply trucks, hating the students who swan in and out. That's what I did at a big studio in Delhi. Nobody spoke to me. Not a *namaste* or a smile. It was like being invisible."

Zohra and he were just about surviving, mainly on the money she earned from work at a bookshop. They had the same conversation again and again in those days:

"I want to go back . . . to Moti Block. To my old job at the library."

"We'll get ourselves killed. Who is there to go back for, anyway?"

"My birds. My friends. My rooms. Chinna."

"Chinna is happy where he is. Your grandfather is gone. Your rooms were rented. Your aunt and cousins hate you for marrying me. What if they try to take you away?"

"You're crazy. We're married. They won't do anything now."

"They know us there. Taatha and Akka are still there. You think they'll wait for us with welcoming garlands, don't you?"

And so the argument would carry on into the small hours, until they were too tired to talk.

"The first few years were not like they are in the movies," Elango said with a wry grimace.

Things had changed for them only two years ago, he said, when Sudhakar got back in touch. He had been through a long illness, had thought it would kill him, but he had lived to smoke another Charminar and drink another rum. Now with Sudhakar supporting him again, Elango's fortunes had been transformed. Miracles did happen—he had always known that. He was an instructor at a studio in Delhi; he had started exhibiting his work again. He taught, and he made his giant urns and animals, which Zohra carved with words in Urdu when he needed her to. They were always the same words:

> Ride your wild runaway mind
> All the way to heaven.

Last year they had a baby. "I'll make sure he doesn't become a potter," Elango said. "And I'll damn well make sure he is an atheist."

It should have embarrassed him to tell me many of these things. About the way Zohra and he had met, how they had fallen in love, their subterfuges for every rendezvous. His loathing for Akka who had fed them to the wolves. It was as if he had a lifetime of talking to finish in five days and I listened without stopping him. That time when he knew me as a child stretches a strong, invisible web between us in this foreign country where we are surrounded by strangers. I know he never would have spoken to me in this way if I had visited him in Delhi. He and I have met here as two people who can dimly glimpse each other across a river of years and when he speaks to me of his own past he makes it a story that is as far-fetched as myth and intimate as a love letter. He speaks of it with objectivity and without shame. He could be talking about someone else, someone he knows well but no longer feels the need to protect.

I listened, and became better over those days at judging when to allow a silence to lengthen so that he felt the need to fill it, and when to nudge him with a question. I've decided I'm going to write about him—I have to do it, now that I've read the bland notes about him that this gallery has produced. Nobody knows him and his work as I do. Here, they understand nothing of the ancient tradition of terracotta pottery he comes from, how it has been in his family and blood for generations, and how unusual he is to have reinvented himself from those roots. These were the things I told him to convince him about my writing project and he replied with a dismissive shrug and a mocking smile. Then overnight, he agreed, with no explanation.

Though Elango remembered most things with a fair degree of clarity, his memory tripped him up now and then. He sometimes faltered, "I'm not sure. Tell this any way you like, but tell it. Fill in the gaps. Work with whatever earth you get. A potter knows how to do that." Sometimes he meandered, driving me mad with his perverse insistence on talking about everything other than his past, instead making up his "Once long ago" stories. On one of those five days he did not want to say a word, he wanted only to work and commanded me too to make a few honest pots for a change. I didn't argue. I sat at a wheel alongside his, feeling the clay rise and fall between my fingers, waiting. Sooner or later, over the hum of the wheels, I knew I would hear the start of words from him. When his need to remember by telling came around again, I listened and recorded and wrote, even if he went on for an hour, appearing to bring some of the words out with such deliberation that I could almost see them travel a tortuous route from his heart and brain through his vocal cords, twisting up in his tongue, emerging to stand in a logical line with the others.

Tonight as I sit myself down in my room to write up my notes, I try to square the old version of Elango stored away in me with this unfamiliar, mercurial one. Although I want to find out all I can about him, I'm not sure I want the playful, bright-eyed fixture of my childhood to be changed for me. Knowledge alters things forever, he knows that too, but he doesn't appear to care. He might not have spoken to me with his unsettling honesty had he not been far from all he had known, unable to unburden himself to anyone—and then a girl who shared his language as well as momentous bits of his past turned up out of the blue.

So I, often wretched and sorrowful, bereft of my homeland, far from noble kinsmen, have had to bind in fetters my inmost thoughts.

Why has that snatch from "The Wanderer" been lodged inside me so long after I plodded through it for my classes? Is it because I too feel an exile in this English world of English words?

I wish I could go back to London and be there for the firing of Elango's horse. Now that we have met again, he promises to remain in touch. But if I want to see him I have to go to Delhi; he swears he will never return to Kummarapet or to the place that was once our town.

I think he has decided not to come back because the black ink floods his veins at the idea of meeting Chinna again. He refused to look at a picture of Chinna when I took it out to show him. But I left it on a counter and when I came back, it was gone.

Thursday, January 17
More than three weeks since I've had time to write, but this evening was so odd I need to put it down. I was on my way back late from a tutorial and was walking to my room through my college's endless corridors. They are the insides of a spiraling shell, concentric circles—hypnotic, beginning at the ending

and ending at the start. From the entrance you can see an infinity of glass doors growing smaller in size down cinnamon-colored carpeting. The doors swing heavily shut and open, they are functional and understand exactly what's what, they know they must keep fires contained, noise cordoned off—so it was only after I pushed open one of the doors that I heard the sound I couldn't identify. Then saw a figure flat on the floor. Karin. She was stretched full length, face to the carpet. She slammed a fist into the carpet, crying over and over again, "Miranda, Miranda. Come out. I didn't mean it, I didn't." Her sobs were like gasps for air.

I now know who Miranda is. She's the dark-haired girl in round glasses who reads Derrida and Cixous in the French, or so I think because she was checking them out ahead of me in the library queue just that morning. We've talked a couple of times and I've seen her and Karin cycle off together in the early morning, but I know her most of all as someone who flashed a red light off and on and off again when we were singing from our windows at the start of last term. Miranda is on the college rowing team. I went to watch her in a race once and remember the way Karin screamed and jumped as if leaping on a trampoline when her boat approached. After the race we'd all gone off for a drink and I'd seen them together, flushed and boisterous, sitting very close.

Miranda did not make a sound tonight, nor did her neighbors. Karin's cries bounced off the walls of the corridor, but nobody wanted to know what was going on. Miranda's door stayed shut and so did the row of doors down the corridor. I stood there for long minutes of frozen indecision, then turned away as well. She would not want me to pick her up off that floor and cart her back to her room; no rescuer could get away unscathed for coming upon her this way, flattened by a grief so private. I retreated the way I had come, through a series of all-knowing glass doors. I walked all the way round to the other side of the college building to climb into my room through my window that gave onto a courtyard.

Friday, January 18

Until I made myself coffee and brushed my teeth this morning I was locked into the dread of a dream in which Karin, Elango, and Chinna were being burned alive inside a horse on fire. I took my cup, stood at my window, trying to calm down. The light was hesitant, it was just about seven. After a few minutes Karin came into view, wheeling out her bicycle in the cold drizzle. All kinds of competitive races are on their way toward her, traps laid to test her athletic prowess. She needs to float over quicksand to hold on to her scholarship. Her father's letters arrive in her pigeonhole every week, she says, demanding progress reports, the times she is clocking. She ran the 400 meters and the 800 and came back some days ago from her practice session despondent, saying she had broken a speed record. I can't believe it didn't make her happy deep inside, but it was certainly not for long.

"I won't tell my father about it," she said. "He's waiting for something like this. Next stop: the Malaysian Olympic team with him as my coach. I'm his ticket to money and fame. I'd rather be dead."

This morning she did look somewhat dead, and not at all like a record smasher. Her feet dragged, her shoulders drooped.

It didn't surprise me when I came upon her sitting alone at dusk on the bleak walkway that connects one wing of our college halls to another. She was smoking, although her coach makes a fuss each time he smells tobacco on her. When I came closer I saw her eyes were glassy with tears. She looked up at me as I approached and for a moment she stared unseeing, as though she didn't know me. And then she whispered something so softly I had to ask her to repeat it.

"I'm scared," she said.

I stood next to her, wondering what to do, that maybe I should put a hand on her shoulder, then I remembered her reaction to Darius's touch. I sat at a distance, further down the same bench, and waited.

"I'm scared," she said again. "I don't know who to talk to. I can't understand anything."

"About what?"

"What's happening to me. If I go back home and they get to know . . ."

"Get to know what?"

"They kill people at home for this . . ."

"How will they know?"

"One of the other Chinese girls might . . . they're laughing at me. Miranda told someone . . . and now it's everywhere. How could she? Didn't it mean anything to her?"

"You are not going back home," I said. I could not think what else to say.

We sat and smoked in silence. I couldn't leave her there, neither did I know how to help. Where she had been eager to share every detail about Darius with me, she was now watchful and secretive, divulging nothing. We had never laughed about her and Miranda together and everything I thought I knew was guesswork.

The chill of the open walkway sent its tentacles through my jacket. I thought of the fiery afternoon in Elango's courtyard when I had made my first real cup. I recalled each detail: the red chilies drying on the roof of his shed, the butterfly that rested briefly on my cheek, Akka giving me a laddu studded with raisins. In an effort to warm myself I tried to imagine—to really feel—the heat of my hometown in the summer when we were like parched birds in search of shade and water.

But here only a damp alien cold that had many fingers and could prize through every layer of clothing and creep underneath. My mind was still in London with Elango and I wondered if at that moment he was walking the city alone in his oversize jacket, searching for things he would not find. A meal he could eat with his fingers. His wife, his baby. The dog he had abandoned. The lightning tree by his pond. The bushy long hair that had seemed an essential part of him had gone, taking with it the wild merriment with which he infected us as children in his auto-rickshaw. I thought how unlikely it was that I had found him here, on a new continent, when I had thought I would never see him again.

In the quadrangle, some kind of night bird started to call and the sky glowed as if the clouds were reflecting light. Across the courtyard, sliced into pieces by the bare arms of a beech tree, Miranda's window was yellow with light.

After her long silence, when I had almost forgotten why I was sitting on a bench with a cigarette stub between my fingers, Karin said, "Once my brother ran away from home after my dad beat him with a bamboo cane. You know why he beat him?

Because my brother gave me a harmonica. He'd told me not to play it when my dad was around, but I forgot and when my dad caught me playing it, I put all the blame on my brother. He didn't come home for five days."

"I ran away from home once. But only down the road. Nobody even noticed," I said with a gloomy sigh.

"You must have been gone for just five minutes." She began to giggle and lit another cigarette. With some difficulty because of her trembling hands.

The lights in the rows of windows began to be blotted out as curtains were drawn. Music from different rooms floated into the air, mingling into a concert. In Miranda's window I could see someone moving around, brushing hair, placing books in a pile, pausing for a long moment, until suddenly there was a black square where the lit window had been. I could tell that Karin's eyes were focused on that window as well. The open walkway we were sitting in had the laundry rooms on one side and the stairs to the dining hall on the other, with the porter's lodge next to it, and was invaded by the smell of detergent and boiled potatoes each time the swing doors opened. Shivering students with their hands tucked into sweater sleeves began to appear in ones and twos, headed for dinner in the hall. Karin picked up her little heap of cigarette stubs, took mine, and went across to the dustbin.

Turning toward me again, she seemed to have gone through a transformation. She began to do heel kicks. Her long green coat flapped at her calves and her hair swished from side to side. She grinned. "Come on, let's go eat chili con carne and apple fucking crumble again." She shoved her beret onto her head and began to sing "Parsley, Sage, Rosemary, and Thyme" in a falsetto. Two boys sprinted past us down the corridor; one of them leaped in the air, managed to touch the ceiling, whooped with joy.

"I want to meet your Indian man, your potter," Karin said. "Did you find him in London? In fact why don't we find you a man? You still haven't had sex *once*."

She chattered on, a knot of boys came through the doors and she paused to talk to them. We turned toward the steps of the dining hall and were about to climb them when Joe Wintergreen, the porter on duty, called out to her. He didn't like her, she had told me at the start of term. She said he held back her letters and did not give her the messages people left for her. I haven't told her I once overheard him calling her Miss Wonton instead of Miss Wang as he placed a call for her to our corridor phone through the switchboard.

"Miranda Walker has just asked for a change of room— wants to move right out to college housing on Rose Lane," Joe said, smirking. "You wouldn't know why that is, would you, miss?"

Maybe Karin delivered him a retort that would sting for days. I didn't hear her. I didn't stop for her. I was already racing back down the walkway to my room for my wallet and bicycle keys. It was blindingly obvious suddenly and I raged at myself for not thinking of it earlier. Friday the 18th has come. I know Elango's flight is in the early hours of the 19th. I can't let him fly home before I see him again. I shot down the hill faster than I ever used to with Karin in those early wild days, pedaling furiously as if my legs were pistons. If I made it to the last train, I might be able to reach him before he left his hotel. I threw my bike into the station's parking area and ran to the ticket counter.

As I write this, my wide, worried eyes stare back from the

window glass next to me. I look out into the blur of dark trees and twinkling lights in passing towns, wishing the train would go faster, would not stop for every nondescript town on the way, as if my entire, confused life depends on this journey. "I want to meet your Indian man, your potter," Karin had said. I don't know if I will make it before he leaves, and if I do, I don't know if he will want to see me. But having found him by such chance, how can I let him leave—just like that? If I reach his room in time, I can send the boxes of chocolates for Zohra and my mother that I bought at the station shop. That's reason enough to see him. Maybe I can go with him to the airport. A few extra hours. That's all I want.

Saturday, January 19

In the darkness of the car on the way to the airport last night, I sat without speaking, and so did Elango. The driver, who might have been the chatty kind at an hour less ungodly, drove without conversation after his initial question about our terminal number. I looked out of the window at the dazzle of sky-high billboards, dazed and sleepy in the warmth of the car after my rushed journey, lines from a poem running through me on a loop. *I started Early—Took my Dog—And visited the Sea—The Mermaids in the Basement—Came out to look at me.* A few hours earlier I had been with Karin on the way to the dining hall, and a few hours before that, in the morning, I had been at a poetry supervision. It now seemed a lifetime away. I wasn't the same girl who had cycled down to Dr. Farrell's and taken my place at the table, watching as he completed his methodical laying out of five pieces of cake, five cups for tea, a squat round teapot with Earl Grey tea bags, and five sheets with copies of the same poem.

But no Man moved Me—till the Tide Went past my simple Shoe—And past my Apron—and my Belt And past my Boddice—too—

Every week, Dr. Farrell waits for us to read the poem he's picked and respond to it. His goatee, his reticent manner, the way he never meets our eyes, makes me wonder at times if he would even know me if we ran into each other on a street. He listens to us with his head bent toward the table as if that's where our words come from, and gives us barely perceptible smiles if we say anything he considers intelligent. That morning I was pleased with myself for extracting one of his smiles and nods. I hadn't known how the poem I had taken apart and analyzed would settle inside me by the evening. I must have been whispering it because I heard Elango: "Are you saying something?"

"No, no . . . I wasn't."

"It's very late. You needn't have come to the airport. It'll be the middle of the night by the time you get back to your town." He turned away and looked out from his window. I could tell there was annoyance, barely concealed.

"It doesn't matter. I wanted to . . ."

I shouldn't have come, I thought, and that had been clear to me the second I burst into the lobby of his hotel. It was a bad idea. I had been flung onto the reception area through the revolving doors and found Elango there, wrapped in the blue anorak and a woolly scarf. He was startled to see me, and not in a good way. I had fumbled with chocolate boxes and explanations until we were in the car the gallery had sent to take him to the airport. It was already past one in the morning, a Friday that had turned to Saturday, and knots of people stood around street corners drinking. At first we made forced small talk about the city and the gallery where he had been teaching. But once we reached the motorway there was nothing but the hum of the car and rushing darkness.

And He—He followed—close behind—I felt His Silver Heel Opon my Ancle—Then My Shoes Would overflow with Pearl—

"There was no need to come," he repeated. "Still it's good you came, I had forgotten something."

He began riffling through his backpack, turning over things inside it, swearing softly when he could not find what he wanted, and then all at once he was holding a hand out toward me.

And made as He would eat me up—As wholly as a Dew Opon a Dandelion's Sleeve And then—I started—too—

"What is this?" I said.

"Open it and see for yourself." He switched on the light inside the car and all of a sudden I could see him, leaning over toward me. Watchful eyes. The start of a smile.

Inside an elegant rectangular wooden box with sturdy brass clasps were slots with tools—trimming tools with sharp metal loops and slim polished handles, wooden ribs curved into different angles, worn on some edges. There were tools I didn't recognize: wooden knives, paddles, knobs. Carving tools with pointed blades. I touched them, I picked one or two out from their slots, put them back.

Elango turned off the light and sank into the backrest. "A Korean potter gave them to me when I was about your age. They are yours now."

"But don't you use them? How can I take them from you?"

"I do, but I have others . . . and I can get more . . . now that

I travel. Usman Bhai used the carving tools from this set for the calligraphy on the first horse. Zohra . . . she has her own. Doesn't want to use these . . . they have bad memories for her."

He went quiet again at the memories that made Zohra want never to touch these. I wondered what she had done with the other tools with painful associations: her grandfather's bamboo quills, his ink pots. I hadn't been able to ask Elango these questions for fear of sending him into one of his black moods.

"A teacher should pass on something valuable to his student," he said. "This is the best thing I can think of."

The miles were being gobbled, chewed, and digested by the car. Not a single traffic light stopped us, nor roadwork. We went so fast it was as if we were skimming the air some inches above the road's surface. Signs for the airport flashed past the window. It was too soon—too soon for him to leave. A huge black wave of despair came over me. In minutes he would be swallowed up by the doors of the airport. I would have to go all the way back alone, and I didn't know exactly how to do it. I didn't want to leave. I wanted to get onto that plane too, and go home with him, back to people I knew. My mother. Chinna. Even Tia.

I couldn't trust myself to say much, so I mumbled, "I'll look after the tools."

Elango laughed. "They are not for looking after, they are for using."

And then, in the way my father used to talk to Tia and me about plate tectonics, Elango started telling me about the exhibition in Delhi where he had met the Korean potter who later sent him the tools. He described how he had seen the man demonstrate the making of a waist-high pot, building it up patiently, with coil after coil of clay, each coil as heavy as an elephant's trunk. Onggi pottery, he called it. Elango saw the way he beat it into its final shape with a big wooden paddle—the ones in the box were miniatures by comparison—and how, after the pot was made, the Korean potter danced to loud music as he threw, slapped on, and painted colored slips onto the pot, as if he were in a trance. Much later, many layers of slip lathered the pot, and the potter was covered head to foot in clay, sweat, colors. Elango had watched, riveted. He understood then how you have to immerse yourself—quite literally—body and soul to make anything worth making.

I didn't know when I would hear again these intonations and words, this particular language of my childhood. I listened as if my life depended on remembering every word.

The signs for the airport grew larger, planes flew low over-head, billboards appeared, Elango kept talking. We unloaded his suitcase, the car left, and we took stock of bay numbers, departure times, gate numbers, carts. By the time we reached the gates toward the security check, beyond which I would not be allowed, I was able to summon up a smile of sorts. He walked away, his blue anorak and dark backpack became one of many jackets, coats, luggage, goodbyes, and I felt a huge suffocat-ing charge of tears starting somewhere deep inside me. Gritted my teeth, tried to turn myself to practical matters. How to get back—would the Underground be working at this hour—should I spend the night at the airport?

I felt a light hand on my shoulder and Elango was there again. He took his woolly scarf off and draped it over my neck. "You need that more, in this cold country," he said. And then he was gone.

I got back to my university on a morning train, after a night on airport chairs. It's now Saturday evening. The town was quiet this morning, everyone was sleeping off Friday. Too bleary-eyed and dazed to trust myself on a bicycle, I left it at the station and trudged through shortcuts back toward my college. I lurched down one of the bridges over our narrow river, pausing to lean on the parapet when I felt my head swim. The willows that had wept green and then yellow into the river were bare-branched in the new-washed light of the pale morning. On the horizon, water and sky could hardly be told apart. Bicycle bells rang and voices called indistinctly to each other. I heard the crunch of more footsteps on the bridge and turned to look. Darius had appeared, walking with two others, from whom he detached himself to come to me.

"What's happened? Are you okay?"

His words came out as tentative as always. He stood beside me, leaning on the parapet as his friends went on ahead without him. He put an arm around my shoulder and said, "Come on, let's go get some hot chocolate, shall we?" His tall, ungainly body bent down toward me and I leaned into him as if he were a wall.

Wednesday, January 23

Karin has been back at the pottery studio every day, for the first time since those early weeks when we met. She arrives, shoves her coat onto a hook, flings her muffler over it, glares at her fingers, and attacks her nails with her teeth. After this she is fiercely unsociable for the next two hours, making pots, then she cleans the slop off her wheel, washes and dries her tools, returns them to their slots—and she's gone. Not a word all through—no questions about where I went that evening when I left her without warning on the walkway, or about my Indian potter. No further confidences about Miranda.

Thursday, February 14
She was back at the studio for many days, and has stopped coming just as suddenly. It turned out she had been making identical round-bellied vases with narrow necks. Once her pots were leather-hard she started working on them with carving tools. She covered her shelf with a damp dishcloth when she left each day and went back to the studio to work on them again. Now they are fired and finished and I see she has upturned each of the vases and turned them into faces with stereotypical Chinese features: slanting eyes, snub noses. She's used glazes and stains and given them red blush marks on their round cheeks. She has stuck real hair, her own, onto their heads.

I suppose I was not the only one in the studio wondering what she was doing. I saw the others who use the pottery glance in her direction, then quickly away. At home, everyone would have peered over her shoulders and asked her a dozen questions. Here, curiosity is bad manners.

A few minutes ago, one of Miranda's housemates in Rose Lane, an American called Jake, rolled his eyes heavenward and told me that "my friend Karin" was a "nutter." He said that for the whole week before Valentine's Day, Miranda has been receiving beautifully packed boxes, containing pots in the shape of human heads, hair and all. They come with rolls of paper that have a typewritten message. One word. Jiaying. Yingtai. Dongmei. Qingzhao. Liling. Each one a Chinese female name.

Saturday, February 16

Earlier tonight I bumped into Karin at a party in the next-door college—we were seeing each other after quite a gap. It was a no-reason party, just a weekend thing, a "let's-forget-everything" party because this term is already like eternity, dull and grim and going straight into exams in the next term. There were fairy lights strung up from the trees and music and warmth and people flowed out from the room where the food and drink were. The alcohol and frenzy made it possible for the cold to be forgotten. The music boomed loud enough for the bass to be felt and heard by your muscles and bones and I stood at an outer edge holding a plastic cup of wine, watching the dancers on the broad, solid table that had been set outside. Karin was on it, dancing with Darius. It was as though their bitter parting at St. Ives had never taken place. Between her knee-high boots and short skirt was an expanse of skin that he could not keep his hands off. She stumbled and giggled and clowned. She drank, she jumped down to chatter with me. There was no mention of Miranda or Chinese clay dolls. She reminds me of one of those colored fountains that shoot skyward, dramatic and gorgeous, die down leaving no trace other than a few nondescript spigots, then rocket up again. It was as if she had been turned on and would keep going until she collapsed. The emerald glitter on her eyelids sparkled, the snow gleamed blue and white. My first real snow.

Elango's woolly scarf was wrapped twice around my neck and the scent of him that clung to it, of smoke and aftershave, made me dizzy with wanting to be away from here and in London again—though I knew that London no longer had him. He was back in Delhi, reunited with his child and with Zohra. It must be cool and sunny there, rose-ringed parakeets swooping in flocks over the bright gardens that are scattered around that city, and they probably spent the day in the sunshine and at night curled up under thick blankets, swearing never to be parted again.

I took the scarf off and stuffed it into my bag.

Karin hopped off the table, shouted something over the music, wandered off again. We eddied and flowed around the gardens and the rooms inside, losing sight of each other in the half-dark parts of the lawns, finding each other again. We were smoking by a snow-laden bench when a lanky boy passed us. His dark hair was puffed up like a well-risen loaf and he wore a jaunty blue muffler around his neck. I recognized his tone and accent—he was a friend of Darius's whom I had met before, a bony Hungarian who had the air of searching for people to oppress with goodness. Once he had locked me against a doorway for many minutes, grilling me about famines and floods in India as though both were my personal failures. And when Darius had come upon me at the bridge on my way back from the station, they had been together.

The Hungarian looked at me with concern. "I asked Darius about you the next day, I was so worried for you. I hope he made sure you were feeling better."

He turned to Karin, bowed with a hand on his heart. His teeth shone like phosphorus in the darkness. I could see his face angled toward her as he talked but I could not hear a word once the next song started, shatteringly loud. Darius pushed at the snow with the toes of his boots, making a tiny hillock at our feet. After his Hungarian friend left, he did not look up at Karin and she did not say another word to me the rest of the evening. I don't know what she thinks I was doing with her boyfriend, but I can feel the acid in the wine turning my throat and tongue to cardboard.

Wednesday, March 20

Term has ended and the colleges have emptied out. The British students have left for their homes, and those among the foreigners who can afford it have gone away too, for holidays in warmer places. I've been left in the almost empty college building along with a handful of others. I know Karin is around, and we nod at each other in passing but she no longer drops in and flops down on my bed to chatter nonstop as she used to. The doors near my room have stopped banging open and shut, the shuffling of footsteps has ceased. The dining hall is closed.

Never very adept at things to do with food, I've been dealing with the closed dining hall by buying myself a book on Indian cooking, and in a fit of nostalgia, I made dal and rice. For all of the next day the kitchen at the end of my corridor smelled of home. Yutaka, the monosyllabic Japanese boy who has a room on my corridor, crinkled his nose each time he came into the kitchen, and I couldn't tell if he hated the smell or wanted a taste. I didn't offer it to anyone else. I ate it all, with my fingers in the privacy of my room, wishing Elango were there to share my emancipation from the tyranny of cutlery.

Yesterday, buoyed by the success of my first experiment, I decided to go shopping. There is a Pakistani corner shop near a petrol station which I cycle to at odd hours if I run out of cigarettes or coffee. It's at quite a distance, beyond the boundaries of the university. I hesitated for a little while, knowing my bicycle had a flat tire, but then I decided I could not bear to wait till the next day, I would walk in spite of the rain. I made a list of ingredients from the cookbook, put on my thickest jacket and boots, and set off. My father would have smiled. He liked cooking, tried teaching me, but I never cooperated. He used to leave the kitchen a big mess, and each of his cooking sessions would be followed by a ritualistic mock scolding by my mother as she cleaned up. After he died, we found we could no longer sit at the dining table to eat—the two square feet of his empty chair had become a howling wasteland. By unspoken mutual consent, Tia and Amma and I began serving ourselves in the kitchen and eating with our plates on our laps, in front of the TV.

The shop was warm and bright with lights and chatter. Reshma at the till opened a stainless-steel box and offered me kababs. She grinned and said, "Memories of home, eh, now that college is empty?" I browsed the shelves, chewing on the kabab, marveling at my culinary innocence. I hadn't paid the slightest bit of attention before to all the jeera and dhania and masoor and mung on those shelves. They even stocked ghee. I filled my basket, paid, and left. I pulled my hood over my head against the drizzle and started the long walk back, my mind occupied with menus for myself.

I was walking on the pavement between the shop and the petrol station on the corner when the thickset blond man who had been paying for beer ahead of me at the shop went past on his bicycle. As he passed, he slowed down and punched me hard on my shoulder. "Fucking cunt, your curry stinks!" he shouted.

He emptied the last of the beer from his can over my head, tossed the can onto the pavement, and cycled off, thrusting a middle finger into the air.

Despite the force of his punch and the stream of beer down my face, I had not fallen. For a few seconds I didn't move. I saw potatoes roll away down the sloping concrete, wondered why vegetables were trundling about on suburban pavements, then realized that my bag had slipped from my hands and my groceries were strewn all over. I bent down to pick up the spilled things. The tomatoes had gone too far, the packet of rice had split and scattered like sleet on the pavement, and I could not find the coin-size vial of saffron, as precious as gold.

As I write this, I can hardly breathe. It happened so quickly. He was gone before I could move. If he had been on foot as well I would have swung my shopping bag at him and smashed his head with my tins of chickpeas. There was no time—he was gone before I knew what had happened.

This is what I am telling myself—but somewhere inside me there is a rustle that says no, Sara wouldn't do anything, she is a coward, she ran off from school during a riot, forgot her little sister, she was so busy saving her own life.

What was I to do next, after picking up the things I could retrieve? I had to be methodical to keep my fear under control. He might be waiting for me down the road or along the lonely stretch that I had to walk through before I reached the gates of my college. I debated going back to the shop—but what would they do? Surely they would not call the police for something so insignificant—I wasn't injured.

I had wiped my beer-soaked hair with my scarf and pulled my jacket's hood securely over my head so my face was hidden. I began to walk, but it was oddly complicated because my shaking legs kept twisting one into the other. I smelled of beer. People would take me for a drunk if they saw me stagger this way. It was hard not to fall. Past the petrol pump, cross at the traffic lights, then down the line of houses with identical bay windows and lights behind net curtains. The scent of parsley and baking cheese wafted out along one part of the street. A dark smudge of woodland would come up next and I would have to gather courage and hurry past it. The only sound was the swish of car wheels on wet streets. Nobody else was walking on this rainy evening.

I thought of the horse. It protected whole villages from harm. I put my hand into the pocket of my jeans and wrapped it around the small piece of terracotta that I always had with me.

I turned a corner, saw at a distance the house on Rose Lane that Miranda Walker had moved to. Miranda's house was a dark, looming cube with the windows shuttered—every occupant must have gone home. It was an unwritten rule that everyone going home for holidays had to grumble about the oppression of days closeted with siblings and parents, and Miranda had participated loudly in the dining hall when this topic came up. I had seen her leave the next day with a mother in a loose cashmere cardigan, a debonair father who swung her suitcases into the car even as he ruffled her hair, a frantically excited spaniel in the back trying to clamber out of the window. Miranda had not turned back once for a last look, even though Karin was near the college gate, trying to fit a key into the padlock of her bicycle, taking too long over it. Ever since, Karin has been ferociously determined at the library, studying until all hours. She is a year ahead of me and has finals coming up.

Down Rose Lane were more houses owned by my college, all shuttered. Another bicycle swished too close past me and my heart thudded. I moved to the inner edge of the pavement even though overhanging creepers poked me in the face and water dripped from them, droplets somehow getting into my neck. Last term a skinhead had chased Karin down the street, not realizing his prey was an Olympic-class athlete. The memory made me smile. Then my fear came back, and the cold. My beer-soaked hair was turning into an icy helmet.

A whole series of events went through me like bullet shots as I half ran back to college. That last night when Elango had gone out into the rain with Zohra, never to return. How five men had hammered on our door and pushed their way in looking for them, yelling abuse. My bewilderment about why he couldn't come back, why the mob had destroyed his work and burned down his house. The way Chinna had searched for him. His whines and whimpers through the first, sleepless night at our house. The way he kept running off to Kummarapet—only to find that Elango's cottage and workshop were gone too, along with the old moringa tree. There was a pile of ashes and warped metal in what used to be the courtyard, where Taatha's people were already piling construction material.

How Vasu and Revathi came and sat on our doorstep weeping about being driven away out of their house. How Vasu had saved Elango's precious box of Korean tools and given it to my mother to send on—and now the same box was with me, like a talisman passed on from hand to hand.

It was only after forty-five minutes, when I reached my room in college and locked the door, that I dumped my shopping bags on the floor, put my head in my hands, and gasped out two dry sobs of relief. I was still panting when there were knocks on the door from someone down the corridor saying, "Are you going to come? We're starting the movie. It's a Tarkovsky. *Nostalghia*."

I can't understand why I still feel so shaken when I wasn't even hurt by that racist bastard. My head throbs, my throat is dry, I can't get a word out. I want to be at home, home as it used to be when my father was alive, when my mother was strong, when Elango was down the road, when I was small enough to be hoisted by him into his auto-rickshaw. All at once I am back with my father in his hospital room, his eyes concentrations of pain, his mouth gagged behind a ventilator mask. And then it is the monsoon in Bombay and we are waiting for news from the surgeons who are operating on his heart. I am staring out of the big windows at the rain-swept streets and I say to Tia, "I can't stop thinking of the flood after the night when Elango left."

My mother, drowsing on a chair, murmurs, "Hasn't the surgeon come out? It's been so long."

"Go back to sleep, Amma, nothing's happened yet," I say.

I get up and walk to one of the windows, and see that a man outside is struggling with an umbrella that has been blown inside out and upside down in the wind; were I an umbrella, I would be that umbrella. The rain lashes down against the glass to which I am pressing my forehead and it makes no sense that the rain can't wet me though there is only this transparent sheet between us. I wonder why, with my father a few paces away, his ribs sawed in half and chest open, I am thinking about that day a few years ago when I was only thirteen and unable to feel happy even though my mother had told me Chinna was our dog now, because who knew when or if Elango would ever come back.

The rain had drummed down then too. It had not stopped for two days: monotonous, continuous, as if unloosing water onto earth was all the sky had been created for. There was a flash flood because of a dam burst upstream and the river had risen all at once. People who were on the banks had to run to safety as a roaring wall of water crashed onto land. It had flooded the buildings along the bank and swept away shacks and houses. The overflowing pond behind Kummarapet had claimed the remainder of the shattered horse. Elango's shed by the pond was blown away by the wind, and the lightning tree had fallen on its side.

One of the houses the river swallowed up was an archive with a precious store of Urdu manuscripts and books. Its ground floor rooms and basement and shelves went under, along with manuscripts that had been illuminated by hand, back issues of newspapers and periodicals, books of poetry that had no copies, decades of collecting and preserving. They restored many manuscripts later. You need to put wet books in a freezer to save them. There were so many books in the archive that they had to move out bodies from the morgues and put books in their place.

When the water retreated, people went into the inundated archive to rescue what they could. Wading through silt and paper they found Usman Alam inside the building. The blind calligrapher had a desk there long ago, my mother's newspaper reported, and an employee named Sadiq Mehmood said his old teacher had begun to visit again in recent times, wanting to touch and smell the ancient books though he no longer had the eyes to read anymore.

The calligrapher had been found seated at the desk, face down in a book on the table, up to his knees in water. It was clear he had died there, although nobody knew when he had entered the building or why he had not left it when the waters started to rise.

Thursday, May 30

I fell very sick soon after that March evening. The college was still deserted, hardly anyone else down the corridor other than Yutaka and Karin. Not knowing what else to do, I decided to disregard the awkwardness between us and staggered to her room, so dehydrated I could hardly move my arms or legs. She sprang into action, getting me to the sick bay that minute, and after that, for more than two weeks, I was either on fire or freezing. I coughed until my ribs became an aching cage around my chest. The room had a window, but the curtain was drawn and I lost all sense of time. Someone would come in, I was sure of that, and I struggled to open my eyes because I wanted to see who it was, and talk, but although I felt I was awake, I could not move.

By the time I was sent back to my room, in April, the exams were only a few weeks away. I couldn't go to the library and my eyes burned if I tried to read. I could not sit up for long. Karin had her finals in May and had very little time, but she still came twice a day, as if nothing had ever happened to damage our friendship. She would check that I had enough food, and sit for an hour every evening reading to me. I told her it was pointless and all the tutorial essays and notes she was reading aloud were barely registering on my numb and addled brain, but she carried on.

"I believe in osmosis," she kept saying. "Just lie there, don't even try to listen. It will enter you."

She carried on for a whole week, reading out critical essays on Victorian novels and metaphysical poetry. She would pause over unfamiliar words and enunciate them slowly, syllabically—"con-tra-pun-tal," "sub-li-mi-nal," "an-thro-po-mor-phism." She would roll her eyes to the ceiling and exclaim about them. What in God's name was the use of this knowledge? She, at least, was learning to build airplanes.

She left me to my own devices when she thought it was safe to do so, and locked herself up to study. If she got a First, as she planned to, she had the offer of a postgraduate degree in Leiden.

Tuesday, June 18

The exams are long over, and the festivities after them are already history. The summer vacations have just started. We go to the airport, Karin and I, headed for separate flights. Mine goes to Rome, where I meet a friend and start traveling. Her flight is to Amsterdam. She'll spend the summer working at Boeing and then she goes on to her PhD. This time it is not a sports scholarship; she never has to run again.

"Come and see me when you're back here next year?" she says before she walks through the security check gates. She gives me a cheeky grin. "Amsterdam's very chilled out. We'll smoke pot, look at Rembrandt, and live in a barge on the canals. Let's have a fling!" She winks, waves her passport at me, and is gone.

I've given her a mug I made for her. I glazed it deep red and engraved it with Elango's Korean tools. "Osmosis Forever," it says.

The Grand Old Dog of Kummarapet

Chinna was out for his daily stroll down the alley. He liked short ambles now, near the house because he didn't see or hear too well, and one of his legs was stiff, but not so stiff that he didn't give the birds in the backyard a scare if they became too daring. And when the heat season came around twice or thrice a year, some primitive thing inside him still made him restless for the scents and the chase, and he found the strength he thought he was losing.

He had a way of walking exactly the same route each day, sniffing at the same places, moving on. His dark muzzle was dusted with white, the folds of his neck hung lower, and from certain angles his eyes looked like pieces of glass. He was content to wander slowly, make sure all was well, and then come back to the house to observe passersby in the quadrangle from his particular spot on the front veranda.

Throughout the day the woman talked to him. She had nobody else to talk to, the dog could see that. The woman told him about crossword clues and the editor's obsession with a new machine the office had acquired—a computer. It would do away with typewriters, so it was said. She told him Sara had finished with university and begun another degree. In London. At an art institute. Wasn't that wonderful? She told the dog about the river dolphins Tia was studying somewhere in the east. She sang to them, and they came to her. Chinna listened to the sound of the woman's voice and felt a soothing drowsiness come over him.

When he reached the fourth lamp post on his walk, Chinna paused to sniff. He noticed a woman standing a short distance away, toward the end of the alley. A stranger with a smell that came from a bottle. Chinna liked humans who smelled of sweat and warmth and food. He liked to push his nose into crotches to get a stronger sense of them. This woman smelled like plastic and glass. But there was something else. A scent of decaying meat. That intrigued him and he put his nose in the air to get a stronger whiff of it.

She walked down the road toward him. She was in no hurry. Her head was tilted to one side. She smiled at the dog as she came closer.

"Tashi, Tashi," she said. "Come on, let's go home. It's been a long time."

Chinna lowered his head and looked at her. He could not tell what the woman was saying. Mostly he understood words from intonations and familiar sounds. This woman made very little sense, even so, somewhere far inside him something stirred. That voice. Those sounds. It was confusing and alluring, a call to a place within him that had been locked away.

"Tashi, I've got your favorite toy. And a bone." She drew a soft white mass from her bag. A long-eared rabbit. One ear torn. She pressed its belly and Chinna heard a sound that might have been a bird or a mouse. He paid it no mind. He wanted to get at that rotted meat scent.

The woman held out the toy closer to him and took another step toward him. She unclasped her bag and put a hand in. She began to bring something out of it. A small hard object dropped to the ground from the bag and she bent down to pick it up. An ancient gesture that was coded into the soul of every ancestor Chinna possessed—a human who bends to the ground must be watched, he may be picking up something to hurl at a dog. He bared his teeth and gave her a low growl.

He walked away—but slowly. He was who he was, he would not run. He was Chinna, the grand old dog of Kummarapet, who had lived and loved and populated the neighborhood with versions of himself.

He sniffed the nearby lamp post with close attention, raised a leg against it, and looked meditative as his trickle turned to a puddle on the ground. When he had finished, he began to walk home. The daily round was over. He would sit on the veranda for the next hour. A new generation of children would stop at the door and pet him. Some of them would bring sweet biscuits and the mother of the two girls would tell them it was not good for an old dog to eat sugary things. She would sit by him, stroking him now and then, and the familiar scent of coffee would tell Chinna it was almost time for his mutton and rice.

And then a deep, sweet nap during which he would dream of the bushy-haired man who had long ago picked him up in a forest, bathed him in a pond, held him close, and fed him morsels from his own mouth.

Acknowledgments

Rukun Advani is to blame for this book as for its predecessors—none of them would exist without him. His allies, Piku, Soda, Barauni, Jerry, and Biscoot, have been my determined research assistants and Chinna is of their pack.

I could not have written this book without the generosity and fellowship of potters: my first teacher Bani de Roy, who passed on to me the ideas of Shoji Hamada, from whom she learned. Jeff Diehl and Donna Diehl of Lockbridge Pottery, West Virginia, for their utter generosity to a stranger: for teaching me, housing me, and introducing me to the work of the Korean potter Kang-hyo Lee, whose Onggi techniques I knew nothing of before. Thanks also to Manisha Bhattacharya, inspiring guide and much-missed friend; to the potters of Kumartuli in Calcutta, especially Basudeb Paul; to co-students and teachers at Delhi Blue Pottery. Most of all my mother, Sheela Roy, for teaching me to make things before anyone else did.

As I was struggling to give this novel shape, my nephew Abhishek Roy sent me material from the Vedas and Puranas, as well as other leads. It's a kind of miracle when the family baby morphs into comrade and adviser and I'm grateful he is kind to his aged relative.

There is much literature, often conflicting, on the myth of the submerged horse. For an overview I relied greatly on Wendy Doniger's learned essay, "The Submarine Mare in the Mythology of Siva" (*Journal of the Royal Asiatic Society of Great Britain and Ireland*, 1971, no. 1, pp. 9–27). On the "making" side of things, Ed Doherty's online record of the Ayyanar horse-building project at the American School in Chennai was a lifesaver when my research trip was killed by the pandemic.

My thanks to Arvind Krishna Mehrotra for letting me borrow his brilliantly iconoclastic translations of Kabir (*The Essential Kabir*, Delhi, 2011); to Parvati Akki for help with the Telugu; to Haider Zaidi for the endpaper calligraphy, S. A. A. Zaidi, Jennifer Dubrow, and Professor Muzaffar Alam for information on calligraphic techniques; and to Begum Anees Khan for Nasr, the remarkable school she established in Hyderabad. My thanks also to Elahé Hiptoola, my Nasr schoolmate, for her descriptions of Ramzan with Zakiya-Apa. For incisive, helpful comments on the draft, I am grateful to my first publisher in the United States, Martha Levin.

I am indebted to everyone at HarperVia, Hachette India, and Mountain Leopard Press for their wisdom and attention through the publishing process, particularly Rakesh Satyal for infusing the American publication of the book with the passion and flair I've come to see as his characteristic. Thanks also to Maya Alpert and Tanya Fox for their meticulous work on the text and gray318 for the striking jacket design.

In Britain, this was among the first titles at Christopher MacLehose's new Mountain Leopard Press. There is something pleasingly symmetrical about this: my first book was one of his first when he set up MacLehose Press in 2008. To travel with him to his new list underlines how fundamental he is for me as a force in my life, not only the writing part of it.

I am ever grateful to my family and friends for putting up with my demands, particularly Myriam Bellehigue, who read this book's first draft despite a health crisis in her family. When we met as students thirty years ago, we had no idea a long literary partnership was ahead. Without her clear-eyed readings of my drafts, my books would be poorer; without her words, my novels would not exist in the finest possible French translations. This book is for her, with love.

A. R.
Ranikhet, March 2021

Here ends Anuradha Roy's
The Earthspinner.

The first edition of this book was printed and
bound at LSC Communications in
Harrisonburg, Virginia, July 2022.

A NOTE ON THE TYPE

The text of this novel was set in Sabon, an old-style serif typeface created by Jan Tschichold between 1964 and 1967. Drawing inspiration from the elegant and highly legible designs of the famed sixteenth-century Parisian typographer and publisher Claude Garamond, the font's name honors Jacques Sabon, one of Garamond's close collaborators. Sabon has remained a popular typeface in print, and it is admired for its smooth and tidy appearance.

HARPERVIA

An imprint dedicated to publishing international voices,
offering readers a chance to encounter other lives and other
points of view via the language of the imagination.